# NOT FOR SALE

BY
## SANDRA MARTON

MILLS & BOON

First published in Great Britain 2011
Harlequin Mills & Boon Limited,
Eton House, 18-24 Paradise Road, Richmond, Surrey TW9 1SR

© Sandra Myles 2011

ISBN: 978 0 263 88645 0

Harlequin Mills & Boon policy is to use papers that are natural, renewable and recyclable products and made from wood grown in sustainable forests. The logging and manufacturing process conform to the legal environmental regulations of the country of origin.

Printed and bound in Spain
by Litografia Rosés, S.A., Barcelona

# NOT FOR SALE

# CHAPTER ONE

LUCAS VIEIRA was mad as hell.

His day had not gone well. Not gone well? Lucas almost laughed.

An understatement.

His day had been chaos. Now, it was rapidly turning into catastrophe.

It had started with a mug of burned coffee. Lucas had not even known there could be such a thing until his P.A.—his very temporary P.A.—had brewed a pot of something black, hot and oily and poured him a cup of it.

One taste, and he'd shoved the thing aside, flipped open his cell phone to check his messages and found one from the same fool of a reporter who'd been badgering him for an interview the past two weeks. How had the man gotten his number? It was private, as was the rest of Lucas's life.

Lucas cherished his privacy.

He avoided the press. He traveled by private jet. His two-level penthouse on Fifth Avenue was accessible only via private elevator. His estate on the ocean, in the Hamptons, was walled; the Caribbean island he'd bought last year was festooned with No Trespassing signs.

*Lucas Vieira, Man of Mystery*, some wag had once called him. Not exactly true. There were times Lucas couldn't avoid cameras and microphones and questions. He was a multi-billionaire, and that stirred interest.

He was also a man who had risen to the top in a profession where lineage and background had significant meaning...

And he had neither.

Or, rather, he did—but not the kind Wall Street generally preferred. Not the kind he would discuss, either. The only questions he would ever consider were those that concerned the public face of Vieira Financial. As for how Vieira Financial had come to be such a powerhouse, how Lucas had come to be such a success at thirty-three...

He had tired of being asked, so he'd finally offered a response in a recent interview.

"Success," he'd said, in his somewhat husky, lightly accented voice, "success is when preparation meets opportunity."

"That's it?" the interviewer had said.

"That's it," Lucas had replied, and he'd unclipped the tiny mike from the lapel of his navy wool Savile Row suit jacket, risen to his feet, walked past the cameras and out of the studio.

What he would never add was that to reach that point, a man could permit nothing, absolutely nothing, to get in his way.

Lucas frowned, swung his leather chair away from his massive Brazilian rosewood desk and stared blindly out the wall of glass that overlooked midtown Manhattan.

Which brought him directly back to today, and how in God's name was he going to keep to that credo?

There had to be a way.

He had learned the importance of letting nothing come between a man and his goals years ago when he was a boy of seven, a dirty, half-starved *menino de rua*—a kid living on the streets of Rio. He picked tourists' pockets, stole whatever he could, ate out of restaurant trash bins, slept in alleys and parks, although you didn't really sleep when you had to be alert to every sound, every footfall.

There was no way out.

Brazil was a country of extremes. There were the incredibly rich who lived in homes that defied description, and the incredibly poor, the *favelados*, who eked out an existence in the *favelas*, the shanty towns, that clung to Rio's hillsides. Lucas was not even one of them. He was nothing. He was vermin. And what seven-year-old could change that?

All he had was his mother. And then, one night, a man she'd brought home took a look at Lucas, trying to make himself invisible in the corner of their cardboard shack, and said forget it, he was not going to pay good money to lie with a *puta* while her kid watched.

The next day, Lucas's mother walked him to the dirty streets of Copacabana, told him to be a good boy and left him there.

He never saw her again.

Lucas learned to survive. To keep moving, to run when the cops showed up because they'd as soon beat the crap out of you as not. Then, one night, somebody yelled, *"Bichos!"* but Lucas couldn't run. He was sick, half-delirious with fever, dehydrated after vomiting up what little was in his belly.

He was doomed.

Except, he wasn't.

On that night, his life changed forever.

Some do-gooding social worker was with the police. Who knew why? It didn't matter. What did matter was that she took him to a storefront that housed one of the few organizations that saw street children as human. There, they pumped him full of antibiotics, gave him fruit juice to drink and, when he could keep that down, food. They cleaned him up, cut his hair, dressed him in clothes that didn't fit, but who gave a damn?

The clothes were free of lice. That was what mattered.

Lucas wasn't stupid. In fact, he was bright. He'd taught himself to read, to do math. Now, he attacked the books they gave him, observed how others behaved, learned to speak properly, to remember to wash his hands and brush his teeth, to say *obrigado* and *por favor.*

And he learned to smile.

That was the hardest thing. Smiling was not a part of who he was, but he did it.

Weeks passed, months, and then there was another miracle. A North American couple showed up, talked with him for a little while—by then, Lucas had picked up passable English from one of his teachers—and the next thing he knew, they took him to a place called New Jersey and said he was now their son.

He should have known it wouldn't last.

Lucas had cleaned up nicely. He looked cute. Black hair, green eyes, golden skin. He smelled good. He spoke well. Inside, though, the boy who trusted no one was still in charge. He hated being told what to do and the New Jersey couple believed children should be told what to do, every minute of every hour of every day.

Things deteriorated rapidly.

He was not grateful, his would-be father said, and tried to beat gratitude into him. His heart was owned by demons, his would-be mother said, and demanded he seek salvation on his knees.

Eventually, they said he would never be any good. On his tenth birthday, they drove him to a hulking gray building and handed him over to Child Services.

Lucas spent the next eight years going from foster home to foster home. One or two were okay but most of them… Even now, as an adult, his fists knotted when he thought back to some of what he and others had endured. The last place was so terrible that at midnight on the day he turned eighteen, he'd tossed the few things he owned into a pillowcase, slung it over his shoulder and walked out.

But he had learned what would become the single most important lesson of his life.

He knew precisely what he wanted.

Respect. That was it, in a word. And he knew, too, that respect came when a man had power. And money. He wanted both.

He worked hard, picked crops in New Jersey fields during the summer, did whatever manual labor he could find during the winter. He got his GED—his General Educational Diploma—because he had never stopped reading and reading led to learning. He enrolled in a community college, sat through classes when he was exhausted and desperate for sleep. Add a helping of socially acceptable good manners, clothes that fit the long, leanly muscled body of the man he had become, and the way to the top suddenly seemed possible.

More than possible. It was achievable.

At thirty-three, Lucas Vieira had it all.

Almost.

Almost, he thought grimly, on this day that had started with bad coffee and an inept secretary, and he had no one to blame but himself.

Anger surged through him and he shot to his feet and paced the length of his big office.

A bad sign, that uncharacteristic show of fury. Learning to contain one's emotions was also necessary for success. Still, it wasn't as bad as his having missed the signs of his current mistress's unrealistic reading of what she'd called a relationship.

When he'd thought about it at all, he'd called it an affair.

Whatever it had been, he was on the verge of disaster.

He was going to lose buying Leonid Rostov's twenty billion dollar corporation. And the deal was close, tantalizingly close to finalization…

Everybody wanted the Rostov holdings but Lucas wanted them more. Adding them to his already formidable empire would validate everything he had worked so hard to become.

A few months ago, when word got out that Rostov might be selling, that he was coming to New York, Lucas had taken a gamble. He had not sent Rostov letters or proposals. He had not phoned the man's Moscow office. Instead, he'd sent Rostov a box of Havana cigars—every photo of the Russian showed him with a cigar in his teeth—and a business card. Across the back he'd written, *Dinner in New York next Saturday, 8:00 p.m., the Palace Hotel.*

Rostov had swallowed the bait.

They'd had a leisurely meal in a private room. There was no talk of business. Lucas knew Rostov was sizing him up. Rostov ate heartily and drank the same way, Lucas ate sparingly and made each drink last. At the end of the night, Rostov slapped him on the back and invited him to Moscow.

Now, after endless flying back and forth, negotiating through translators—Rostov's English was chancy but how could Lucas fault it when his Russian began with *zdravstvuj*—hello—and ended with *dasvidaniya*?

Now, Rostov was in New York again.

"We have one more meal, Luke-ahs, one bottle of vodka—and then I will make you happy man."

Only one problem.

Rostov was bringing his wife.

Ilana Rostov had joined them the last time Lucas was in Moscow. She had a beautiful if surgically altered face; diamond earrings dangled like Bolshoi chandeliers from her ears. She moved in a cloud of choking perfume and she was fluent in English; she'd served as her husband's translator that night.

She'd also had her hand buried in Lucas's lap beneath the deep hem of a crisply starched tablecloth.

Somehow, Lucas had made it through the meal, the translator he'd hired for the evening oblivious, Rostov oblivious, only Lucas and Ilana Rostov aware of what was happening. He had barely escaped with his dignity, never mind anything else, intact.

And Rostov was bringing her with him tonight.

"No translators," he'd said firmly. "Translators are functionaries of the state, *da*? You can, of course, bring a voman. But for talking, my Ilana will take care of you as good as she will take care of me."

Lucas had almost laughed. And he *could* laugh this time, because he had an ace up his sleeve.

Her name was Elin Jansson. Elin, born in Finland, spoke flawless Russian. She was a model; she was Lucas's current mistress. She would be his date, his translator…

And his protection against Ilana Rostov.

Lucas groaned, went to the window wall behind his desk and pressed his forehead against the cool glass.

It had all seemed so simple. He should have known better. Life was never simple, and today had proved it.

"Mr. Vieira?"

Lucas swung around. His temporary P.A. smiled nervously from the doorway. She was young and she made lousy coffee but far worse, no matter what he did to make her feel comfortable, she remained half-terrified of him. Right now, she looked as if one strong gust of wind might blow her over.

And well she should look exactly that way, he thought grimly. He had left orders that he was not to be disturbed.

"What is it, Denise?"

"It's Elise. Sir." The girl swallowed dryly. "I knocked but you didn't—" She swallowed again. "Mr. Rostov called. I told him you were unavailable, just the way you said. And he said to tell you that he and Mrs. Rostov might be a few minutes late to meet you and—"

Her voice trailed off.

"You've told me," Lucas said crisply. "Is there anything else?"

"I just—I just wondered if—if I should phone the restaurant and—and tell them there'll be only three for dinner.'"

*Merda!* This was going from bad to impossible. Did the entire world know what had happened?

"Did I ask you to do that?"

"No, sir. I just thought—"

"Don't think. Just do what you're told." The girl's face collapsed. Hell. So much for controlling his emotions. "Denise. I'm sorry I snapped at you."

"It's Elise," she said in a wobbly voice. "And you don't owe me an apology, sir. I just— I mean, I know you're upset…"

"I am not upset," Lucas said, forcing a smile the way he'd done when he was a boy. "Why would I be upset?"

"Well—well, Miss Jansson—when she was here a little while ago—" Another gulping swallow. "Mr. Gordon was at my desk. And we couldn't help but hear— I mean, I couldn't stop Miss Jansson from going by me and then, once she got inside your office…"

"So," Lucas said, through his teeth, "I had an audience." He attempted a smile but suspected it was more a grimace. "What about everyone on the other floors? Were they in attendance, too?"

"I don't know, Mr. Vieira, sir. I could ask around, if that's what—"

"What I want," Lucas said, "is that you never mention this again. To me or anyone else. Is that clear?"

The girl nodded.

*Mental note,* Lucas thought dryly. *Offer to quadruple regular P.A.'s salary when she returns from vacation if she swears never to leave her desk again barring death, disease, or God forbid, marriage.*

"It is, sir, and I want you to know how sorry I am that you and Miss Jansson—"

"Go back to your desk," Lucas snapped. "And do not interrupt me again or you'll find yourself at HR, collecting your final check. Understood?"

Apparently, it was. Denise, Elise, whoever in hell she was, slunk off, shutting the door behind her. Lucas glared at it for a couple of seconds. Then he sank into the chair behind his desk, tilted it back and stared at the ceiling.

Wonderful. In a couple of hours, he'd be meeting with a man who spoke little English and a woman who only wanted to get her hands inside his fly. He had no translator, and now his private life was the topic of discussion among his employees.

Why wouldn't it be?

Elin had made one hell of a scene, storming in, demanding to know about "that blonde bimbo" as she tossed a photo on his desk. It had appeared online, on some gossip site, she said. One look and Lucas knew it was a Photoshopped miracle but done so carelessly that the "bimbo"—an actress, the text said—seemed to hover next to him, her feet a few inches off the ground.

He'd looked up, already smiling, a second away from telling Elin exactly that. Then he'd looked at her icy eyes, the grim set of her mouth, and inconsequential annoyances suddenly began to add up.

Elin's little makeup bag, left in a vanity drawer. The jeans, shirt, and sneakers left in his closet. So she could get out of a cab at her place at seven in the morning, she'd purred, without raising eyebrows.

*Stupid*, he'd thought, *worse than stupid!* Elin didn't care about raising eyebrows. Besides, half the women in Manhattan got out of cabs in the early morning, still dressed as they'd been the prior night.

And maybe the most obvious part of that lie was that he could count on one hand the number of times Elin, or any other woman, had slept in his bed the entire night.

He wasn't into that. Sex was sex; sleep was sleep. You did one with a woman. You did the other alone.

"You think it's funny that you sneaked around? That you cheated on me?" Elin had slapped her hands on her hips. "I'm waiting for an explanation."

That did it.

Lucas had risen to his feet. Elin was tall but at six-three, he towered over her.

"I do not cheat," he'd said coldly. "I do not sneak. And I do not explain myself. To you or anyone else."

She had grown very still. Progress, he'd thought, and he'd gone on, calmly, to remind her of how things were between them. That they were having an affair and it was enjoyable, but—

She'd screamed something at him. In Finnish, but still, he could tell what she'd said was not complimentary.

A second later, she was gone.

No big thing. That was what he'd thought. In fact, it was long past time they said goodbye to each other…

And then, reality had come rushing in.

The dinner. Leonid Rostov. His wife. For one wild second, Lucas had imagined going after Elin and asking if this meant she wasn't going to go with him tonight…

He stalked to the built-in rosewood cabinet across the room, bypassed Denise-Elise's witch's brew, opened a sliding door and took out a thin Baccarat highball glass and a bottle of Macallan single malt Scotch.

It was all his fault. He should have known better than to mix business with pleasure but it had seemed perfect. A beautiful, sophisticated woman who would know which fork to use even as she translated Russian into English and English into Russian. Where in hell could a man find a woman like that at the eleventh hour, even in New—

"M-M-Mr. Vieira?"

"Damnit," Lucas snarled, and swung toward the door. His P.A. was trembling. Beside her stood, hell, Jack Gordon. Lucas had hired him a year ago. Gordon was bright and innovative. Still, there were times Lucas wondered if there was more to Gordon than met the eye.

Or maybe less.

Lucas jerked his head. Denise-Elise stepped back and closed the door, and Lucas turned an icy look on Gordon.

"This had better be good."

Gordon blanched but he held his ground. Lucas had to admire him for that.

"Sir. Lucas. I think, when you hear what I have to say—"

"Say it and then get out of here."

Gordon took a breath. "This isn't easy…" He took another breath. "I know what happened. You and the Jansson woman… Wait a minute, okay? I'm not here to talk about that."

"You damned well better not be."

"She was supposed to go with you tonight. To that meeting," Gordon said hurriedly. "You mentioned it Monday morning, how Rostov didn't want real translators, so he'd talk through his wife and you—"

"Get to the point."

"Sir. I know someone who's fluent in Russian."

"Perhaps you weren't listening to everything I said on Monday," Lucas said with icy precision. "Rostov refuses to have anyone he thinks of as a functionary present tonight. He says that's what official translators are, and perhaps they are, in his world, but what it comes down to is—"

"Dani can pretend to be your date."

Lucas's mouth twisted. "I don't think I can fool our Russian friend into thinking I've suddenly decided to go in for boys."

"Dani's a girl, sir. A gorgeous girl. She's smart, too. And she speaks Russian."

Lucas felt a flare of hope. Then he faced reality. A girl, sight unseen? For an evening as important as this? No way. For all he knew, he'd be compounding what was already a mess into a disaster.

"Forget it."

"Sir, it would work."

Lucas shook his head. "It's clever, Jack, but this is a twenty billion dollar deal. I can't run the risk of this woman screwing things."

Gordon laughed. Lucas's eyes narrowed to emerald slits.

"Did I say something amusing?"

"No, no, of course not. Look, I've know Dani for years. She's exactly what you need for a situation like this."

"And if I were foolish enough to say yes to your suggestion, she would do this because…?"

"Like I said. We're old friends. She'd do it as a favor to me."

A muscle flickered in Lucas's jaw. A twenty billion dollar deal, hinging on a man who drank too much vodka, a woman who had more limbs and libido than an octopus and a woman he'd never met?

Impossible.

*And impossible to pass up.*

"All right," he said sharply. "Call her."

Jack Gordon's eyebrows rose. "You mean it?"

"Isn't that what this conversation was all about? Call her. Tell her—"

"Dani. Dani Sinclair."

"Dani. Tell her I'll pick her up at seven-thirty. Where does she live?"

"She'll meet you," Jack said quickly.

"The lobby of the Palace. Eight o'clock sharp. No. Make it ten of the hour." That way, he'd have time to hand the Sinclair woman cab fare and get rid of her if she turned out to be totally wrong for the job. "Tell her to dress appropriately." He paused. "She can do that, can't she?"

"She'll dress appropriately, sir."

"And, of course, make it clear I'll pay her for her time. Say, one thousand dollars for the evening."

He could see Gordon all but swallowing another laugh. Yes, Lucas thought coldly, why wouldn't he find his employer's predicament amusing? If this worked, he could take credit for saving Lucas's corporate ass. But oh, if it didn't…

"That sounds fine, sir." Gordon held out his hand. "Good luck."

Lucas looked at the outstretched hand, fought back a sense of repugnance he knew was foolish and accepted the handshake.

Jack Gordon hurried back to his own office before he pulled out his cell and hit a speed dial digit.

"Dani. Baby, have I got a deal for you!"

He explained as quickly as possible; Dani Sinclair was not one for long conversations but then, that wasn't what men paid her for. When he'd finished, he heard the slow exhalation of her breath.

"So, let me get this straight. You told some guy—"

"Not just some guy, baby. Lucas Vieira. *The* Lucas Vieira. The guy with more money than God."

"You told him I'd give him a date?"

"Yeah. Only, not that kind of date. This is dinner with Vieira, a Russian guy and the guy's wife. You need to act like you and Vieira are a thing. And you need to translate." Jack laughed softly. "I guess taking a degree in Cyrillic languages was a good idea after all."

"I'm taking my Master's," Dani Sinclair said, "and a girl has to think about her future." She paused. "How much did you say he'll pay?"

"A thousand."

Dani laughed. "Did you forget my going rate, Jack? It's ten thousand for the evening."

"Baby, we go way back. Elementary school. Middle school. High school."

"Fine. I'll give you a special discount. Five thousand."

"Jeez. For a meal?"

"And, of course, my usual fee if your Mr. Vieira wants anything else."

Jack Gordon rubbed the top of his head. "If he wants more, you can negotiate the fee yourself."

Dani chuckled. "Jack, you wily fox. You haven't told him about me. What, you want him to be shocked?"

"I want him to owe me," Jack Gordon said, his tone suddenly cold. "And he will, no matter how this goes."

"Charming. Okay, so when does this happen?"

"I thought I told you. Tonight. The Palace lobby. Ten minutes of eight."

"Oh, but I…" Dani fell silent. Five K to eat a fancy meal, talk some Russian and in between, pretend she was the date of Lucas Vieira, the gorgeous, sexy, take-no-prisoners Wall Street tough guy. And a minimum of ten K if he ended up wanting to prolong the evening.

So tempting. If only she could do it. Trouble was, she already had a date for tonight, with a Texas oilman who came through the city once a month like clockwork.

There had to be a way…

"Dani?"

And there was. She could clear, say, forty-five hundred without doing a thing besides making a phone call.

"Yes," she said briskly. "Fine. The lobby, the Palace, ten of eight."

She disconnected, checked her cell's contact list and hit a button. A female voice answered on the third ring, sounding breathless and a little rushed.

"Caroline? It's Dani. Dani, from the Chekhov seminar? Listen, sweetie, I have a translating job that I don't have time to take and I thought, right away, of you."

Caroline Hamilton used a hip to shut the door of her Hell's Kitchen walk-up, then tucked her cell phone between her ear and her shoulder, shifted the grocery bags she held so she could free a hand and secure the door's three locks.

Dani from the Chekhov seminar? Caroline tried to picture her as she made her way across the six feet of floor space to what her landlord insisted was a kitchen. Yes, okay. Dani, a fellow Master of Arts student in Russian and Slavic Studies. Tall, stunning, dressed in the latest designer stuff. They'd never spoken except to say "hi" and "see you next time," and to exchange numbers in case one needed to check with the other about an assignment.

"Caroline? You still there?"

"I'm here." Caroline eased the grocery bags onto the counter, took a Lean Cuisine from one, worked at opening the little tear strip on the box while still keeping the phone at her ear. "A translating job, you said?"

"That's right. An unusual one. It involves dinner."

Caroline's belly rumbled. She had passed on lunch. No time, less money. The phone slipped as she finally got the container from the package. She grabbed it before it hit the Formica counter.

"...as the pretend G.F. of a rich guy."

"What?" Caroline said, reading the directions. Three

minutes on high, peel back the liner, stir, another minute and a half—

"I said, it's dinner. You meet this hotshot business guy at the Palace Hotel and you pretend you're his girlfriend. See, there's another couple and they speak Russian. Your guy doesn't, so you'll translate for him."

Caroline put the Lean Cuisine into the nuker, shrugged off her jacket, pushed her thick, straight-as-a-stick mane of no-real-color hair back from her face, blew strands of it out of her hazel eyes.

"Why would I pretend I'm his girlfriend?"

"You just would," Dani said, "that's all."

Caroline punched in the three minutes. "Thanks but I'll pass. I mean, it sounds, well, weird."

"One hundred bucks."

"Dani, look…"

"Two hundred. And that meal. Then the night's over, you go home with two hundred dollars in your jeans. Except," she added hurriedly, "except, of course, you can't wear jeans."

"Well, that's that, then. I definitely don't have—"

"I'm a size six. You?"

"A six. But—"

"Size seven shoes, right?"

Caroline sank onto the rickety wooden stool that graced the counter. "Right. But honestly—"

"Three hundred," Dani said briskly. "And I'm on my way. A dress. Shoes. Makeup. Think of what fun this will be."

All Caroline could think of was three hundred dollars. You didn't need to be a linguist to translate that into a piece of next month's rent.

"Caroline! I need your address. We're running out of time here."

Caroline gave it. Told herself to ignore the prickly feeling dancing down her spine, told herself that same thing again, two hours later, when Dani spun her toward the mirror and she saw...

"Cinderella," Dani said, laughing at Caroline's shocked expression. "Hey, one last thing, okay? Let this guy think you're me. See, the friend who set this up thinks I'm gonna do the date, I mean, be the date, and it's easier all around if we keep it that way."

Caroline looked at her reflection again. Dani's fifty-dollar-a-bottle conditioner had taken her hair from no-color to pale gold. Her hazel eyes glittered, thanks to the light sparkle of gold shadow on her lids. Her cheekbones and mouth were a delicate pink and her dress... Cobwebs. Slinky black cobwebs that showed more leg than she'd ever shown except in shorts or a swimsuit. And on her feet, gold sandals, their heels so high she wondered if she'd be able to walk.

She didn't look like herself anymore, and something about that terrified her.

"Dani. I don't—I can't—"

"You're meeting him in half an hour."

"No, really, it just feels wrong. To lie, to pretend I'm you, that I'm this Luke Vieira's girlfriend—"

"Lucas," Dani said impatiently. "Lucas Vieira. Okay. Five hundred."

Caroline stared at her. "Five hundred dollars?"

"We're running out of time. What's it gonna be? Yes or no?"

Caroline swallowed hard. And said the only thing she could.

She said, "Yes."

# CHAPTER TWO

LUCAS went home, showered and changed clothes. White shirt, blue tie, gray suit. A little casual, a little businesslike. Now, all he had to do was calm down.

The hotel was fiftieth and Madison and he lived on Fifth Avenue, only a couple of blocks away. There was no need for his car; like any New Yorker, he knew the fastest way to cover that distance was to walk.

Besides, walking might give him time to tame his temper. He'd snapped at his driver on the way from the office to his condo; he'd barely responded to the doorman's pleasant "good evening, Mr. Vieira," he'd scowled at his housekeeper in response to a simple question.

He was breathing fire, and what for? Ultimately, he was the one responsible for this mess. Why turn his anger on everyone else?

He'd made a mistake, not recognizing that Elin was trying to make more of their affair than it ever could be, but the way to recover from a mistake was to learn from it and move on.

The Palace's elegant lobby was crowded. Lucas found a relatively clear space that gave him an unimpeded view of the entrance, then checked his watch. It was seven forty-five. On the chance Dani Sinclair might have arrived early, he scanned the room for a late-twenties, tall woman with light brown hair, blue eyes and what Jack Gordon had slyly described as "a body that just won't quit" when Lucas had phoned him for a description an hour ago.

"A total babe," he'd said, with a low laugh. "Built for action, if you get my drift."

Lucas's mouth twisted. He didn't like Gordon's increasingly smarmy tone, and he had no interest in knowing if he and the woman had been intimate. As long as she looked presentable, seemed credible as his date and spoke Russian, he'd be satisfied.

There were lots of women in the lobby, some that met Gordon's description, but none were alone as Dani Sinclair would be. If she ever showed up. Frowning, Lucas checked the time again. Four minutes had gone by.

Another slipped past.

Lucas folded his arms, felt a flicker of apprehension. She was late.

It was not a good start.

At five of eight, Lucas could feel the muscles in his jaw tense. Yes, Rostov had said he and his wife would be late but if the Sinclair woman didn't show up soon—

A woman entered the lobby. She was by herself. Lucas felt a surge of hope until he realized this couldn't be the woman he was waiting for. Nothing about her fit Jack Gordon's description.

Her hair was pale gold, not brown. He couldn't tell the color of her eyes from here, only that they were wide-set, like a cat's. Her face was oval, her mouth a soft pink.

Even at a distance, she was stunning.

Feminine. Delicate. Curves gently accented by an incredibly short, clinging silky black dress, long legs that lent sexiness to already-sexy gold sandals with stiletto heels. An erotic image flashed into his head. This woman, wearing only those heels and whatever wisp of silk she had on under that amazing dress…

He scowled.

What kind of nonsense was this? He was here on important business. Besides, it would be a while before he'd want to be with a woman again. The thing with Elin had left a bad taste.

Still, he lifted his gaze, took one last look at the woman's face…

And found her staring at him.

For a heartbeat, their eyes met and held. Lucas felt something knot, deep in his belly. He took a step forward—and then her gaze swept past him and the moment, whatever it had been, was over.

Hell.

He needed a break.

He'd finish the Rostov deal, clear up a couple of other things and then he'd go out to his house in the Hamptons for a long weekend. Alone. Just him and the sun and the sea. Three, four days like that and he'd be ready to get back to work, and to women.

All he had to do was wind things up tonight—except, how was he going to do that? His watch read five after eight.

No question about it.

Dani Sinclair had been a mistake.

Lucas ran his hand through his hair.

He could call the Rostov suite. Plead sudden illness. No. That was the easy way out. More to the point, he wanted things settled, tonight. His only real choice was to go through with the dinner plans, let Ilana Rostov do all the translating, try to ignore her fingers in his lap and if things got bad enough—

"Excuse me."

If things got bad enough, say to hell with it and tell Rostov that he needed to leash his barracuda of a wife…

"Sir? Excuse me."

A hand fell lightly on his arm. Damnit, what now?

"Yes?" he growled as he swung around… And saw the blonde with the cat's eyes looking up at him. This close, he could see that her eyes were hazel, that she was even lovelier than he'd thought.

A woman on the prowl. New York had more than its fair share of assertive women. Or she might be a high-priced call girl. New York had plenty of those, too, and though places like this did all it could to discourage them, they were around.

Either way, he wasn't interested. He liked assertive women but not tonight, with a deal like this on the agenda. And if she was a so-called working girl, even an expensive one…

Forget it. He'd never paid for sex in his life and he never would.

"I—ah, I wonder if you—if you—"

"No. I would not."

She flinched. Hell, she turned pale. Lucas felt a twinge of guilt. She wasn't a pro. And he was behaving like an ass. It had been a long day and it was going to be an even longer evening, but why let it out on her?

"Look," he said, "you're a beautiful woman. I'm flattered that you'd like to have a drink, dinner, whatever—"

"No," she said quickly, "that's not—"

"I'm meeting someone. On business. Your timing is off, okay?"

Those hazel eyes turned cold.

"You have an interesting opinion of yourself, mister."

Lucas raised his eyebrows. "Hey, I'm not the one who—"

"I'm not interested in a drink. Or dinner." The woman drew herself up, steel suddenly in her spine and in her voice. "Actually, I'd sooner have drinks with—with SpongeBob Squarepants than someone as rude and self-centered as you."

Lucas blinked. Then, despite himself, he laughed.

"Thank you."

"For what?" She tossed her head and strands of her hair fell against her cheek. He fought back the insane desire to take those strands between his fingers and tuck them back behind her ear. "And what's so amusing? Do you like having people tell you what you are to your face?"

"No one ever does," he said. "No one would dare."

Her smile was sweet enough to make his teeth ache. And to make him grin.

"What a pity."

"You're right. I owe you an apology. I'm in a bad mood but that's no reason to take it out on you."

He could see her trying to decide whether or not to accept his request for forgiveness. Suddenly, it seemed important that she would.

"Truce?" he said, holding out his hand.

She hesitated. Then her lips curved in a smile. She put her hand in his and he could have sworn he felt a jolt of electricity.

"Truce."

"Good." He smiled back at her. "Look, this really is a bad time. Why don't I give you my card? Call me tomorrow. Better still, give me your number and—"

The blonde tugged her hand free.

"You don't get it." The steel was back in her voice. "I'm not trying to—to pick you up. I'm supposed to meet someone here. On business, the same as you."

Lucas's eyes narrowed. "A man?" he said slowly. She nodded. "And what does he look like?"

"Well, that's just it. I don't know. I mean, I've never met him. But I'm pretty sure he's middle-aged. And probably, well, probably not very good-looking. And... Why are you looking at me like that?"

"What's this middle-aged, homely guy's name?"

The blonde's chin lifted. "I don't think that's any of your—"

"Is it, by any chance, Lucas Vieira?"

Her mouth fell open.

"Ohmygod," she said, "ohmygod!"

"Don't tell me," Lucas said slowly. "You can't be…Dani Sinclair?"

The woman looked as if she might faint.

"You're right," she said. "I can't be Dani Sinclair. But I am."

Impossible, Caroline thought.

No. Not impossible.

Insane. This entire thing, from the minute Dani had called her, right up until now.

*This* was Lucas Vieira? This tall, dark-haired, absolutely spectacular hunk? She'd noticed him instantly. And she wasn't the only one. The lobby was crowded. It was a Friday night, warm even for early June, and it seemed as if everybody was out for the evening.

There must have been a couple of dozen women milling around with their dates, their husbands and boyfriends, and from what she'd been able to see, every one of them managed to shoot little assessing looks at the gorgeous guy standing all by himself.

He'd been watching the door, as if he was waiting for someone.

Okay, she'd thought. He was alone, he *was* waiting for someone.

But he couldn't be Lucas Vieira.

A man who looked like that wouldn't need to hire a woman to pretend to be his date. True, there was more to it than that, Lucas Vieira needed a date who could translate Russian—even more bizarre, really—but whatever the situation, this was not her guy.

*If only he was…*

And, even as she'd thought the words, she'd realized his eyes were focused on her. Her heart had thumped; she'd felt a rush of heat in her breasts, in her belly, in her blood. It went with the way she'd been feeling since leaving her apartment, as if she had stepped into a different reality, assuming another woman's identity, wearing her clothes, about to meet a stranger and pretend she was his girlfriend…

The stranger's eyes had seemed to narrow. He'd taken a step forward.

Caroline had torn her gaze from his and set out blindly through the crowd, heading anywhere but in his direction. She had to concentrate on finding Lucas Vieira, but how to identify him? Dani hadn't described him beyond saying he'd be alone and that he was incredibly rich.

The "incredibly rich" tag could probably be hung on most of the men in the lobby, but none of them were alone—except for the one whose eyes had blazed with fire when he'd looked at her.

Could he be the guy she was supposed to meet? Unless she'd missed something, he was the only man by himself. And he'd been watching the door with such intensity…

There was only one way to find out.

She'd taken a deep breath. And another. Then she'd walked up to him, said "excuse me" as politely as possible… Someone had jostled her. She'd teetered on the ridiculous heels. The stranger's hand—Lucas Vieira's hand—had closed around her elbow, steadying her. She'd already teetered once tonight, getting into the cab that had brought her here.

Then, all she'd thought was how huge a sum she'd owe Dani if she fell and tore this dress.

Now, all she could think of was the burn of this man's fingers on her skin.

Her heart began to race. She tried to step back and he caught hold of her hand again.

"Careful," he said. "This mob is like a herd of wildebeest on the Serengeti. They'd trample you before they knew they'd done it."

It was such an accurate description that Caroline laughed.

"That's good. You have to relax. We won't be able to pull this off unless you're at ease with me."

Her smile faded. This was business. How could she have forgotten that, even for an instant?

"You were supposed to be here twenty minutes ago."

Business, for sure. The smile, the charm, the *I'm-male, you're-female* thing had vanished.

"I know. But the traffic—"

"I'd wanted a little time for us to get a feel for each other."

She already had a feel for him. Not just rich but disgustingly rich. Not just good-looking but fantastically good-looking. Charming when he wanted to be, bitingly cold when he thought that would work better.

Oh, yes, she had a feel for that kind of man.

Her mother's kind.

Not rich like this, of course. You grew up in a small town at the end of nowhere, the men with all the money and power owned the Chevy dealership. The gas station. The shops on what really was called Main Street. And none had been as handsome as Lucas Vieira but the basics were the same.

Too much money, too much power, too much arrogance. Mama had always fallen hard for men who were rich and good-looking and one hundred percent no-good.

Caroline had never understood it. Mama was bright. She was logical about everything else; you had to be, to raise a child without money or a husband. Still, she'd fallen for the same kind of guy over and over.

One good thing was that Caroline had learned from Mama's

mistakes. She'd avoided boys like that in high school, in college, here in New York.

So, what in hell was she doing tonight?

She could never pull this off. Pretend to be Lucas Vieira's date. His girlfriend. Anybody's girlfriend, in a setting like this.

"Mr. Vieira," she said, rushing the words together, "I think I've made a mistake."

"I agree. But the people we're meeting haven't shown up yet, so—"

"I shouldn't be here. I'm not—I'm not going to be very good at this."

"You'll be fine."

There was a grim quality to his voice. He was desperate, but how could a man like this be desperate? He could snap his fingers and damned near every female in the place would come running. Okay. He needed a translator. She could, she supposed, be that, but she could never pull off pretending to be involved with him.

"I can translate for you. But the rest—"

"The rest is the most important part."

Caroline frowned. "I don't get it. Why would me pretending to be your date be important?"

"Not just my date." His mouth thinned. "My lover. My mistress." His hand moved up her arm to her shoulder. She could feel the heat of his fingers on her bare skin. "We'll need to convey a sense of intimacy, Dani. Do you understand?"

She blinked. Dani? Right. Right. That was her name tonight. She was Dani. Oh, if only she were! She had no idea what Dani did when she wasn't in class but there was a sense of sophistication to her that suggested Dani would know how to deal with a man who looked like this. Who sounded like this, that faint, sexy accent, that husky tone of command. A man whose scent was clean and masculine and crisp, if you could call a scent "crisp."

And when had they moved closer to each other? She didn't recall that happening but, somehow, it had, close enough so she had to tilt her head back to look into his face.

"Dani. Do you follow what I'm saying?"

"Intimacy," she said, her voice trembling.

"Yes."

"But why? If this is a business dinner—"

He hesitated. To her surprise, faint stripes of color appeared on his cheeks. He shrugged his shoulders and she thought, *why, he's almost human!*

"The man I'm doing business with has a wife. She's—she's an unusual woman. Very assertive. Make that aggressive. When she wants something, she goes after it." The color in his face deepened. "No matter what that something is, no matter if that something reciprocates or not—"

"She's hitting on you?"

"You, ah, you might say she's…" He paused. "Damned right, she is. And I'm counting on your presence to stop it."

Caroline swallowed hard. "Mr. Vieira—"

"Lucas."

"Lucas. That just cinches it. I can't—there's no way I could—"

"Damnit!"

He was staring over her head. The expression on his face went from harsh to grave.

Caroline stiffened. "What?" she said, and tried to look back, but his hand tightened on her shoulder.

"No. Keep looking at me."

"But—"

"It's the Rostovs. The people we're meeting. They're coming toward us."

If he'd said Genghis Khan's army was thundering out of

the steppes at that moment, she couldn't have felt a greater flash of terror.

"This is not good, Mr. Vieira."

"For God's sake, it's Lucas. Lucas! Mistresses do not call their lovers by their surnames!"

"But I'm not your mistress. I don't want anyone to think I'm your mistress." Caroline could hear the rising panic in her voice and she took a steadying breath. "I don't believe in women being mistresses. In them being property. In being owned and supported and—and held as chattel by men, and—"

"Luke-ahs!"

A meaty hand slapped Lucas on the shoulder. The man that went with it was meaty, too. "Enormous" was a better word, Caroline thought. He had small eyes, a big nose and a grin that stretched from ear to ear.

"Leo," Lucas said. "It's good to see you again."

Leo Rostov's gaze slid to Caroline.

"Ah. This is your voman."

"No," Caroline said, "I'm—"

"Yes," Lucas said with a little chuckle that had no connection to the pressure of his fingers digging into her flesh as he slipped his arm around her waist and brought her to his side. "But she's one of the 'liberated' women, Leo, if you know what I mean. She'll bristle if you call her 'my woman.'" He looked down at Caroline. "Isn't that right, sweetheart?"

Was that a note of desperation in Lucas Vieira's voice? A glint of it in his green eyes? Well, he'd got himself into this mess. How he'd done it was anyone's guess but he could damned well get himself out of—

"Luke-ahhhs!"

A woman slipped from behind Rostov's bulky figure. One look, and Caroline understood everything. Ilana Rostov was stunning. Big hair. Big breasts. Big diamonds.

And from the way she looked at Lucas, she was, without question, a cougar on the hunt.

"Luke-ahhhs, oh Luke-ahhhs, you darling man. How lovely to see you again."

"Ilana." Lucas's arm tightened around Caroline. "I'd like to introduce my—"

"Howdoyoudo?" Ilana said, without taking her eyes from Lucas. Smiling, batting her lashes, she stepped in front of him, her face upturned, her breasts touching his chest. "A kiss, darling. You know that is how we Russians greet old friends." Smiling, she rose on her toes and wound her arms around his neck. Lucas jerked back but it didn't matter. Nothing was going to stop her.

Not true, Caroline thought. Something could, and would. Her spiked gold heel, nailing Ilana Rostov's instep.

Ilana shrieked and stumbled back. Caroline threw her a look of abject innocence.

"My goodness, did I step on your foot? I am so sorry!" Swinging toward Lucas, taking the place Ilana Rostov had vacated, Caroline looked up at him. The expression on his face was priceless; it took all her effort not to burst into giggles, but why spoil things now? "Lucas? Sweetie? I'm thrilled to meet your friends but what about dinner?" Still smiling, she moved closer, until they were a breath apart. "I'm absolutely starved, darling."

She watched the swift play of emotions across his face as surprise gave way to sheer delight—and then to something darker, deeper, and far more dangerous. His arms went around her. She spread her hands flat against his chest, felt the strong, steady beat of his heart.

"Yes," he said. "So am I."

No way was he talking about a meal.

Caroline felt her heart thud. When had he seized control of the game?

"Mr. Vieira," she said, "I mean, Lucas—"

He laughed, bent his head to hers and took hot, exciting possession of her mouth.

# CHAPTER THREE

THAT little slip, Dani calling him "Mr. Vieira," could have been Lucas's undoing.

That was the reason he kissed her. The sole reason. Anything to convince the Rostovs that he and the woman in his arms had an intimate relationship.

Why else would he kiss her? He didn't know her and she didn't know him. He didn't have any wish to know her; he was off women for a while.

Kissing the woman with the pale gold hair and hazel eyes was a matter of expediency. It was meant to establish intimacy, to take the sting out of the way she'd addressed him and that glimpse he'd had of Ilana's raised eyebrows.

And, while he was at it, the kiss was to remind her of her function here tonight.

For those reasons, no other, Lucas took his supposed mistress in his arms and kissed her. It wasn't even much of a kiss, just a light brush of his mouth over hers.

But her lips were warm. Silken. Her little "oh" of shocked breath was warm, too, and tasted of mint. Toothpaste, he thought in surprise, a taste that didn't quite go with the sexy dress, the do-me shoes, and…

And, he stopped thinking.

Everything around him faded. The crowd. The noise. The

Rostovs. It was as if each of his senses was solely concentrated on the woman in his arms.

Lucas drew her closer. Slid one hand to the base of her spine and lifted her slightly, just enough so that she fit the contours of his body while he cupped her face with his other hand.

He felt the soft pressure of her breasts against his chest. The tilt of her hips against his. The delicate arc of her cheekbone under his fingers.

Felt himself turn hard as granite.

His lips parted hers. She made a little whisper of sound and he thought, *Yes, that's it, kiss me back.*

She did. For a heartbeat. Then she stiffened. She was going to pull away.

He told himself, with admirable logic, that he couldn't permit that. If they were lovers, she would be eager for his kisses. Anytime. Anywhere. Not just in bed.

Which made him imagine her in his bed, her hair spilling in golden disarray over his pillows, her eyes hot with hunger as he entered her...

Dani sank her small, sharp teeth into his lip.

*"Cristos!"* Lucas jerked back. Touched the spot with his finger. No blood, nothing but a flash-fire rush of fury.

Rostov roared with laughter. Ilana's eyebrows sought refuge in her hairline. And Dani...Dani looked as if she might turn and run and, damnit, he could not let that happen!

Lucas's life had taught him many lessons. Quick recovery. Damage control. Self-control. He needed all those skills now. Somehow, he managed a smile as he wrapped his hand around the blonde's slender wrist. She'd have to wrestle herself free of his grasp and he was betting she wouldn't let that happen.

"Now, sweetheart," he said, his smile changing, going sexy and intimate, "you know we don't play those games in public."

Another laugh from Rostov. A pause, and then a little sigh from Ilana.

And the best reward of all, the cold pleasure of seeing crimson sweep into his defiant translator's beautiful face.

"No," she said, "we—you and I—we don't pl—"

"Exactly, darling. We don't." She looked as if she were torn between embarrassment and the desire to murder him, and that made it easier for him to tug her closer, curve his arm around her waist and hold her captive against his body. "If you want your reward, you have to wait until the evening ends. You know that, Dani."

He knew the second his message registered. If she wanted his thousand dollars, she'd have to play the role Jack Gordon had crafted for her.

"Understand, sweetheart?"

Her eyes flashed. No embarrassment now, no fear. "I understand completely—*sweetheart*."

Lucas laughed. The lady had guts. He had to admit, he liked that in her. He wasn't accustomed to it. Women rarely stood up to him. Well, not until he ended a relationship and then some of them balked, but flying into a rage wasn't the same thing as standing up to him.

Rostov elbowed him in the side. "Your lady is vildcat, Luke-ahs."

Yes. She was.

She was a great many things. Beautiful. Bright. Skilled in Russian—he had no proof of that yet but, somehow, he felt no reason to doubt it. Add the sweet taste of her mouth, the alluring scent of her skin, the lush feel of her against him and she was an intriguing package, the embodiment of sex and intellect rolled into one.

Except for her name.

It didn't fit her. It was flippant. Unfeminine. And she was neither. She'd be an interesting woman to get to know.

Too bad that wasn't on the agenda.

"You know," he said, glancing at his watch, "it's getting late. Why don't we go straight to the restaurant and have drinks there?"

"Ve vill haff champagne," Rostov said, clapping Lucas on the back, "once we walk over two tiny spots, *da*?"

Lucas cocked his head. Dani rattled off something in Russian, Rostov answered, and she looked at Lucas.

"He means that there are two small areas of concern in the deal you and he have made, and he wants to talk about them."

Lucas smiled.

His plan had worked. Rostov was ready to conclude things, Dani understood the nuances of translating. And seeing her now, cheeks still slightly flushed, hair a little disheveled, eyes glittering, not even Ilana would question their relationship.

He could relax.

All that remained was a final few hours of sociability. Then he and Rostov would shake hands and say goodbye, Ilana would become a bad memory, he'd give Dani Sinclair a check for a thousand dollars and they'd never see each other again.

He'd have to thank Jack Gordon.

This wasn't the disaster he'd anticipated. In fact, it was working out just fine.

Caroline sat across the restaurant table from The Woman With The Frozen Face and wondered how she could have got herself into such a situation.

Two rich men. A woman married to one of them but on the make for the other. And she, the buffer between them.

Actually, that part had worked out just fine.

She still couldn't believe how quickly Lucas Vieira had got

out of the quicksand after she'd bitten him. She still couldn't even believe she'd bitten him!

Hell, he was lucky she hadn't grabbed the nearest lethal object and brained him with it.

Kissing her that way. Pulling her against him. Letting her feel the beat of his heart, the warmth of his body. The swift hardening of his aroused flesh.

Biting him was better than he'd deserved and though she'd been furious at how easily he'd turned the bite into something sexy, she had to admire him for being fast on his feet.

Caroline reached for her champagne flute and brought it to her lips.

And for using the incident to convince the Botox Cougar that they were lovers.

Ilana had bought the entire act. She'd followed Caroline into the loo after they'd taxied to the restaurant and looked at her reflection in the mirror that hung above the elegant triple vanity.

"Congratulations, Miss Sinclair."

"Who?" Caroline had almost said, but she'd remembered just in time.

"Your lover is quite a man."

A blush had crept into Caroline's face. What did you say to that?

"Surely," the Cougar had purred, "he is remarkable in bed."

The mirror had shown Caroline the color in her face going from pink to red.

"He's all right," she'd blurted.

Ilana had laughed. Even the attendant, who'd come to the vanity to provide them with little hand towels, couldn't repress a smile.

"I think he must find your attitude a change from the usual, *da*? The careless way you treat him." The Cougar's eyes had met Caroline's in the glass. "You know, I did not at first believe you were his mistress. You do not seem his type."

Truth time. Caroline had taken a breath.

"Of course I'm his mistress," she'd said calmly. "Why else would I be with him tonight?"

For five hundred dollars, the voice within her had whispered.

Because, no question about it, Ilana Rostov was right. She was, most assuredly, not Lucas's type.

She wasn't the type that belonged in this restaurant, either.

The place was small, intimate and elegant. The patrons were elegant, too. She recognized familiar faces from movies and television and magazine covers. The women were expensively dressed. The men exuded wealth and power.

And almost all of them, men and women, had noticed Lucas, the men with nods and smiles of recognition, the women with glances that could only be called covetous.

More than one woman had looked at her in a way that said she was amazingly lucky to have such a man's attention. And she was. Or she would have been, if any of this was real, but it wasn't. It wasn't, and she had to keep remembering that—and it was difficult because Lucas was so attentive.

And so dangerously, excitingly sexy, even when he and Rostov had dropped into intense conversation over drinks. Ilana had translated for her husband in a low voice. Caroline had done the same for Lucas.

It had gone very well—except for those times he'd posed a question to her, or leaned in, to hear what she had to say. Then he'd brought his dark head down to hers; she'd felt the whisper of his breath on her skin, found herself thinking that all she had to do was lift her head, just a little, and her cheek would brush his, she'd feel the faint abrasion of that sexy five o'clock stubble against her skin.

Even now, with the deal concluded, a second bottle of champagne opened and poured, the danger wasn't over.

Every now and then, Lucas would touch her.

Her hair. Her hand. Her shoulder, when he lay his arm along the back of her chair and brushed his fingers against her bare skin.

It was part of the masquerade, or maybe he wasn't even aware he was doing it. He was a man accustomed to being with women; everything about him made that clear. Either way, it meant nothing. But whenever he touched her—whenever he touched her…

A tremor shot through her. Lucas, who was talking with Rostov but had his hand on Caroline's, leaned in.

"Are you cold, sweetheart? Do you want my jacket?"

His jacket? Warm from his body, undoubtedly bearing his scent?

"Dani? If you like, I can warm you."

Her eyes flew to his. Something glowed in those deep green depths. Was he toying with her? Her heart was trying to claw its way out of her chest.

"Thank you," she said carefully, "I'm fine."

He smiled. Her heart took another leap.

He had the sexiest smile she'd ever seen.

He had the sexiest everything.

Eyes. Face. Hands. Body. And that kiss. That just-for-show kiss… She'd felt it straight down to her toes. The warmth of his mouth, the feel of his hands…

She made a little sound. Lucas raised an eyebrow. "Are you sure you're all right?"

"Yes," she said quickly. "I just—I just can't decide what to order."

"Let me order for you, darling."

She wanted to say "no" but that would have been foolish. Reading Chekhov was easier than reading the menu. Black truffle mayonnaise. Whipped dill. She doubted either had anything to do with what you put on a bacon, lettuce and tomato sandwich, or the kosher dill pickle you'd eat with it.

It was only that saying she'd let him do something personal for her made her feel uncomfortable—

"Dani?"

And that was ridiculous. There was nothing personal about ordering a meal.

"Yes," she said. "Thank you. I'd like that."

Lucas brought her hand to his lips. "Two thank-yous in a row. I must be doing something right."

The Rostovs smiled. That was good. After all, this performance was for them.

She had to keep remembering that.

Her toes curled.

Oh God, she thought again, as the waiter took their orders, she was as out of her element as a hummingbird in a blizzard. Not just here, in these surroundings.

She was out of her element with this man.

She could leave now. She could. She'd done her job. Ilana Rostov was behaving herself. Her translation duties were completed now that, metaphorically, twenty billion dollars had changed hands. Twenty billion! She couldn't even start to envision that amount of money but Lucas had mentioned it with less fuss than Dani had shown about the five hundred she'd pay her for tonight's masquerade.

It was a lie, all of it, and Caroline understood the reason for it. If she'd had the Botox Cougar after her, well, the male equivalent, she'd have done whatever it took to throw her off the trail.

It was just that—that there'd been moments tonight when she'd thought, when she'd wondered, when she'd imagined how it would feel if she really were Lucas Vieira's date, if she were his lover, if the evening would end in a softly lit room with him undressing her, baring her body to his hands, his mouth…

And thinking like that was wrong.

The waiter brought the first course. Just in time. She needed food. She hadn't eaten in hours and hours. No wonder her brain was in meltdown.

Unfortunately, she couldn't swallow much more than a mouthful. She couldn't eat the main course, either. She was sure it had to be delicious. It looked beautiful, nothing like food, but beautiful anyway.

Trouble was, her stomach had gone on strike. *No room for food here*, it said, *butterflies in residence.*

"Lucas." Was that breathless, desperate little voice hers? "Lucas," she said again, and he turned to her. "I—I—"

His eyes searched hers. A muscle knotted in his jaw. Then he took her hand, did that incredible-hand-kissing thing again and looked across the table at Leo Rostov, who was in the middle of telling an endless joke.

"Leo," he said politely, "Dani's exhausted. You're going to have to excuse us."

It was a request but it wasn't. There was a tone of command in his voice. She heard it and she knew Rostov did, too. His ruddy face grew ruddier. Leonid Rostov wasn't accustomed to having someone else call an end to the festivities.

"Lucas," Caroline whispered, "it's okay. If you have to—"

"What I have to do," he said quietly, "is see you home."

For the second time, she saw that her gorgeous, arrogant date was gorgeous and arrogant but that somewhere inside him, he was real.

There was a flurry of activity. Lucas took out his cell phone, arranged for his driver to meet him outside the restaurant. He waved off Rostov's attempt to pay the bill and ordered another bottle of Cristal.

"You and Ilana stay and enjoy yourselves," he said.

And then they were out of the restaurant, into the midnight streets. Lucas turned her toward him.

"Are you all right?"

"Yes. Thank you. I just— I've had a long day, and—"

His hands were warm and hard on her elbows. There was a look of concern on his face. They were standing so close that she could feel the heat coming off him, see that the emerald irises of his eyes were ringed with black.

Caroline shuddered.

"Damnit," he said gruffly, and he took off his suit jacket and draped it around her shoulders.

Just as she feared, as she'd longed, the fabric held his warmth. His scent.

"No," she said quickly, "really, I don't—"

"Let me warm you," he said, just as he'd said a while ago, but this time there was no questioning what she heard in his voice, what she saw in his eyes as she looked up at him.

The world seemed to stop.

"Hell," he said roughly.

She could have asked why he'd said that. Why his voice sounded as if it had been run through gravel. But asking would have been foolish and she had done enough foolish things tonight, starting with accepting Dani's proposal and ending with not walking out of the hotel lobby the second she'd laid eyes on Lucas Vieira.

"Dani," he said, the single word dark with warning, and she made a little sound, took a step toward him and he knotted his hands in the lapels of the jacket and pulled her into the heat, the power of his body.

And did what he'd wanted to do the entire night.

Bent his head. Took her mouth. Kissed her gently and when she whimpered, rose on her toes and wound her arms around his neck. When she opened her lips to his, his kiss deepened, burned hotter than a flame.

"Dani," he said, against her mouth, and Caroline caught Lucas's face between her palms and brought it to hers so the kiss could go on and on.

And on.

# CHAPTER FOUR

A LONG, black Mercedes pulled to the curb.

Lucas got in, held his hand out to Caroline. She took it and he drew her into the limo's dark, leather-scented interior.

It was like stepping into their own world. No lights. No people.

"Take us home," he told his driver, and then the privacy screen went up and they were alone. "Come here," he said roughly, and without hesitation, she went into his arms.

The Mercedes moved swiftly through the dark city streets, a magical craft sailing the seas of a dream. A lover beyond imagining, his lips on hers, his body hard beneath hers as he drew her into his lap.

Wrong, Caroline thought, this was wrong...

"Open your mouth," he whispered. "Let me taste you."

A moan rose in her throat. Her lips parted against his as the limo sped toward Fifth Avenue.

"I've wanted this all night. You, in my arms. Kissing me."

Yes. Oh, yes. She'd wanted it, too, but—

"Dani. God, you're so beautiful.

"No. Lucas—"

"Do you want me to stop?" He drew back, just enough so he could look into her eyes.

Caroline stared at him. What she wanted was to tell him

that she was Caroline, that she was not a woman named Dani...

"If this isn't what you want, too," he said hoarsely, "tell me now."

She shook her head. "Don't stop. Don't stop. Don't—"

He kissed her, and the world went away.

He lived in the sky.

That was how it seemed, with moonlight pouring in through the windows, as if she and he were surrounded by stars that burned in a private universe.

He kissed her in the private elevator that rose to his penthouse, kissed her as he swept her into his arms and carried her to his bedroom, kissed her as he set her on her feet.

He cupped her breast, moved his fingers over the silk-covered nipple that leaped to his touch. A cry rose in her throat; he captured it with his mouth.

She was on fire for him.

"Dani," he said, and together, they fell back against the wall. His mouth ravaged hers; he pushed up her skirt, his hands big and urgent on her skin. She trembled, clasped his face with her hands, offered him her lips, her tongue, her hunger.

He said something in Spanish. Portuguese. She didn't know, didn't care, didn't care about anything but the feel of his hands, his mouth.

Caroline reached for the buttons on his shirt. He tore aside her thong. His hands clasped her bottom; he lifted her and she gasped at the shock of his erection against her.

"Wrap your legs around me," he said gruffly.

She did, and gasped again as he freed one hand, fumbled between them and then...

And then, God, then he was driving into her, hot and hard, silk over steel, stretching her, filling her and it was wonderful, it was terrifying, it was nothing like the one time she'd been with a man, nothing like she'd ever imagined.

The world began to tilt.

"Lucas," she sobbed. "Oh God, Lucas!"

It was too much, too much, too much…

Caroline screamed in ecstasy.

And felt herself fly with him into the molten heat of the stars.

Lucas had no idea how long they'd been standing like this, Dani still in his arms, her legs around his hips, him holding her up, both of them breathing hard while sweat sheened their skin.

Hours might have gone by. Or minutes. He'd lost the ability to think straight.

Hell, that was painfully apparent. A thinking man didn't do what he'd just done. Made love to a woman with all the finesse of a bull moose in rut.

And without protection.

He couldn't believe it.

The twin demons of a bachelor's life. Disease. Pregnancy. Always out there, waiting for some damned fool. Had he been the fool tonight? Even at sixteen, his first time with a woman, he'd been smarter than this.

How could he have let passion override logic?

"—please."

Dani was speaking to him. Whispering, was more like it. She'd buried her face in the crook of his neck, as if she didn't want to look at him. Between that and the sound of that tremulous whisper, he was willing to bet she was upset.

*Merda*, why wouldn't she be?

"Dani," he said softly, "look at me."

She shook her head. Her hair, all that spun gold silk, flew around her face, brushed against his nose and mouth. Even now, he shut his eyes, let the scent and soft feel of it tease his senses.

"Sweetheart. I know this wasn't—"

"Please. Put me down."

There was a faint note of panic in her words. He nodded, lowered her to her feet, gritting his teeth against the swift rush of desire he felt as her body brushed his.

"Dani—"

"You don't understand." She lifted her head; his throat constricted at what he saw in her eyes. "Listen to me, Lucas. What—what I just did. I don't—I don't ever—"

"I *do* understand." He cupped her face, lowered his head until their eyes were level. "This was too quick. My fault. I'm sorry. I meant to do this right." His voice roughened. "But, I wanted you so badly…"

"No." She clasped his wrists. "That's not it. I meant that I—that I—"

"I didn't give you enough time."

Caroline have a helpless little laugh. "Lucas. We aren't talking about the same—"

"We are," he said. "It's my fault."

They were talking about different things, but what did it matter? What was the sense in explaining now? And—and the truth was, after what she'd just done, having sex with a stranger, going wild in his arms…

All things considered, she was willing to go on pretending to be a woman who could do those things without recrimination. He'd never know she was really Caroline Hamilton, not Dani Sinclair. There was no way she and Lucas Vieira would ever see each other again. Their worlds had intersected by accident and accidents didn't happen twice.

"You have the right to know that I'm healthy," he said softly, taking a strand of her hair between his fingers.

She blinked. "What?"

"I'm healthy, sweetheart." He dipped his head, brushed his lips over hers. "Still, I should have used a condom."

The word made her blush, and wasn't that pathetic?

"Are you—" He hesitated.

She felt her color deepen.

"Yes," she said quickly, "I am. I'm perfectly healthy." No lie there. When the last time you'd had sex was three years ago, you could be sure you didn't have an STD.

Lucas shifted his weight, put his hands flat against the wall on either side of her.

"I didn't mean that. I meant, are you on the pill?"

Stupid, she thought, so stupid! She was. She took it to regulate her period, but he didn't have to know that.

"Yes," she said, and wasn't it ridiculous to blush even harder? She'd had sex with a stranger, sex so out of control she'd thought she might die from the incredible pleasure of it, and talking about condoms and birth control embarrassed her.

Pathetic.

"Good. But if anything should go wrong..."

"Nothing will," she said quickly. One more second of this conversation and she was either going to burst into tears or hysterical laughter.

How could she have done this?

And what did she do now?

Lucas had her caged against the wall. One of her shoes was missing. Her thong was a bit of torn silk, caught around one ankle. What was the protocol? Did she search for the lost shoe? Kick off what remained of the thong? Did she say, *Goodbye, Mr. Vieira, and thank you for a pleasant evening*?

A muffled sound caught in her throat. Laughter or sobs? Either would only add to her humiliation and she thought, without any logical reason, that the woman she was pretending to be would probably know how to deal with all those questions.

"Dani?"

"Don't—don't call me that." Caroline swallowed hard. "I mean—I mean, I've never liked that name."

Lucas flashed a smile. "Actually, I don't think it suits you."

"No. I mean, yes. I mean…" Damn. Her overworked emotions made their own choice. Tears rose in her eyes and rolled down her cheeks. "I have to leave," she said, but when she tried to get by him, Lucas caught her shoulders and held her still.

"Sweetheart." His mouth twisted. "Damnit, I've made you cry."

"No." She shook her head. "No, it isn't your fault."

The hell it wasn't. She was crying. Silently, which somehow only made it worse. He put his hand under her chin, raised her face to his. Her mascara was running, her eyeliner, whatever women called that stuff, had smudged into black streaks. She was a mess.

A beautiful, heartbreaking mess, he thought, and he gathered her into his arms.

"I hurt you," he said gruffly.

She shook her head again but he knew better.

"I did. I was too rough, too fast."

"You weren't." Her voice was soft, as was the hand she lay against his cheek. "It's me. It's what I've done, coming up here with you, behaving like—like—"

"Hush." Lucas gathered her against him, rocked her gently in his arms. It took a long time until he felt the rigidity in her start to ease but he went on holding her close. "What happened is nothing to regret. It was—" What? Unplanned. Unexpected. Being with a woman was the last thing he'd imagined he'd want tonight, but he had no regrets. If anything, instinct told him what they'd just shared would be something he would not soon forget. "It was wonderful," he said softly, tipping up her chin. "Incredible. And it's my fault it wasn't like that for you."

"But it was. Wonderful, I mean."

She was blushing. It was— The only word that worked was "charming," especially when the blush was from a woman who'd given herself with nothing held back.

"I'm glad. Still…" He brushed his lips over hers. "Still, I'll bet I can make it even better."

He heard the little intake of her breath. "It's late. And—"

"I want to undress you."

His voice was rough. Just the sound of it made her knees go weak.

"Undress you. Kiss you. Touch you everywhere. Slowly this time. Very slowly." He drew her to her toes, took her mouth in a kiss that sent her pulse soaring. "We can spend the rest of the night getting to know each other."

She met his eyes, lifted a tentative hand to his face again. Which was stronger, the desire to run…or the desire to let what she knew, she *knew* she wanted, happen? He turned his head, captured her hand, kissed her palm, her wrist, her arm, and Caroline had her answer.

"Lucas," she whispered, and she put her hand behind his head, rose to him and kissed him back.

Slowly, he began to undress her, doing this as he should have the first time, drawing out each caress, each whisper of skin against skin, turning her so her back was to him, nuzzling aside her hair, kissing the column of her spine as he undid her zipper.

The dress fell open. She started to catch it but he slipped his arms around her, cupped her breasts, felt the shudder go through her as he did.

He held her that way, his hands on her, until she moaned

his name and leaned back against him. Her bra had a front closure and he released it, let the bit of silk fall away, bit back a groan when her naked breasts tumbled into his hands.

He heard her breath catch. Felt a tremor go through her. He moved his thumbs over her nipples and she made the kind of little sound that left him wanting to turn her to him and bury himself inside her.

But not yet.

He slid one hand over her ribs. Her belly. Put his mouth to the nape of her neck and kissed the fragrant skin. He moved his hand lower. Lower still. She gasped his name, tried to turn but he wouldn't let her, not now, not when his hand was between her thighs, when her heat filled his palm, when he was harder than a man could possibly be and survive.

Concentrate, he told himself fiercely, concentrate on Dani. On the woman in your arms.

Gently, he parted her with his fingers.

Stroked her.

Heard the hiss of her breath. Felt her try to clamp her thighs together to stop him.

Felt her stop fighting him, fighting herself, and, instead, move against his hand.

"No," she said, "no, don't. Lucas. Don't. I'm going to—I'm going to—"

She gave a long, keening cry. The sound filled him with pleasure and he swung her toward him, swept her into his arms and brought her to his bed.

Moonlight from the big skylight overhead bathed her in ivory.

Her hair streamed over his pillow, burnished gold against cream. He had imagined her like this but the reality was more perfect than the mental image. She was lovely. All of her.

And she was his.

He made love to her slowly, as he'd promised, watching

her face as he did, loving the way her eyes widened, her lips parted as he caressed her. When his hand reached her breast, she caught it in hers.

"Let me touch you," he said in a husky whisper, and she released his hand, held her breath, cried out as he feathered his thumb over a dusky-pink nipple, then lowered his head and drew one tightly furled tip into the heat of his mouth.

The taste of her was almost his undoing. Honey. Cream. Vanilla. He sucked her nipples, licked them until her moans told him she was crazy with wanting him…

As he was crazy with wanting her.

"Lucas."

Her whisper was a plea.

He took her in his arms. Lifted her to him and kissed her with slow, thorough deliberation. He couldn't get enough of her; as much as he wanted to sheathe himself within her silken heat, he wanted the kiss to go on and on. She trembled against him and he trembled, too, aching to possess her.

It was sweet torture.

She sighed his name again, this time with growing urgency. Her arms went around his neck. She lifted herself to him, pressed herself to him. He knew what she longed for; he longed for it, too, that hot, exciting release but he told himself he could wait, he could wait…

"Lucas," she whispered, "Lucas, please."

It was the "please" that almost finished him, something in the softness of how she said it, the innocence with which she said it, that nearly sent him over the edge.

He stood, stripped off his clothes, saw her eyes widen when she saw his erection. He was big; he knew that. Big, and proud of it because he was male, but there was a flash of fear in her eyes.

"It's all right," he said hoarsely. "We fit, remember? Just a little while ago."

He took her hand, brought it to him.

Bad move.

Her hand closed around him. He groaned. Her hand moved again and he caught it, held it in his as he opened a drawer in the table beside the bed and fumbled for a condom. Seconds later, he knelt between her thighs.

Slowly, his gaze linked to hers, he entered her.

"Is this good for you?" he whispered. "Tell me it is. Tell me—"

She reached for him. Brought his face to hers. Kissed him, sighed his name, and he lost himself in the kiss, in the rhythm they set, in possession of her.

The world went up in flame.

After a long, long time, Lucas rolled onto his side with her curled like a satisfied kitten in his arms. He liked the feel of her, soft and warm against him.

"Sweetheart? Are you okay?"

She made a sound that was so close to a purr, it made him smile. It was as fine a recommendation as a man could want, he thought as he drew the duvet over them.

"Close your eyes, then," he said softly.

"Mmmm."

Her lashes drifted to her cheeks. He kissed her temple, drew her closer, felt her breathing slow.

Amazing.

He'd ended the day wanting nothing to do with women, and ended the night with a woman in his arms. He couldn't make sense of it—unless wanting her so badly, taking her so slowly was the sexual equivalent of downing a drink in the morning when you woke with a hangover. He hadn't ever had a hangover—getting drunk was a weakness—and he hadn't ever needed sex to forget an affair that had just ended, but anything was possible.

Lucas yawned.

And he was too tired to try to make sense of anything right now.

The illuminated clock beside the bed read three-thirty. They had three hours to sleep until his alarm went off, unless he woke a little earlier and woke her, too, so he could make love with her one more time.

Maybe that wasn't such a hot idea.

Maybe he should have taken her to her apartment, instead of to his.

Maybe he'd regret her spending the night. Look at what had just happened with Elin. She'd spent a handful of nights here and decided it meant their relationship, if you could call it that, had turned serious.

Maybe…

Maybe what he needed was some sleep.

Lucas drew his beautiful translator closer. His eyelids drooped. He smiled a little, remembering that she didn't like being called "Dani," but she'd never told him what she preferred. Danielle? Was that her full name? Somehow, it didn't suit her, either.

He'd find out in the morning.

He'd find out a lot of things in the morning.

The name she preferred. Her address. Her phone number. Because he wanted to see her again. *See* her, not turn this into anything exclusive, of course, although he wouldn't want her seeing other men. He would not tolerate it. He needed his space. He needed his freedom. But—but—

But, he'd work it all out tomorrow. The only possible problem would be if she misinterpreted spending the night in his bed. Women did…

Lucas tumbled into sleep.

And when the alarm rang at six-thirty, there were no problems to work out because Dani Sinclair was gone.

# CHAPTER FIVE

CAROLINE came awake with a start.

In a movie, the heroine would have opened her eyes and come to a slow realization that she was not in her own bed. But this wasn't a movie, it was real life and she knew instantly that she was in a stranger's bed.

There was the enormous size of the bed itself. The faint predawn light, streaming through the arched floor-to-ceiling windows. The skylight overhead. The silk comforter.

Caroline shuddered.

Most of all, there was that hard, warm male body lying against hers, that tanned, muscular arm draped possessively around her waist.

Her heart bumped into her throat.

Scenes of the night flashed through her mind. Throwing herself into Lucas's arms in his limo. Kissing him in the elevator.

Making love against the wall and then in this bed.

Except, it hadn't been love, it had been sex. Trying to turn last night into something soft and romantic was like—like trying to pretend that Madame Bovary was Cinderella.

Useless, pointless, and that she had never done anything like this before, that she looked down on women who went in for hooking up—and that was what this had been, a hook-up, plain and simple—only made it more humiliating.

She'd gone to bed with a man she didn't know and the only good part of it was that he was still asleep.

Sound asleep.

He lay sprawled on his belly, his head turned toward her on the pillow. The duvet had slipped to his waist. Caroline's gaze moved over him.

Even in sleep, he was a magnificent sight.

All that dark, tousled hair. The thick, black lashes that curved against his cheek. The straight nose, sculpted mouth, the tiny dimple in that strong, assertive chin, even the morning stubble on his jaw, was beautiful and sexy.

The comforter was caught just at the base of his spine; she couldn't see the rest of him but she knew, oh how well she knew, that his backside was tight, his legs long, just as she knew that if he rolled over, the rest of him was perfect.

Heat started at the tips of her toes, spread low in her belly, made her nipples tighten.

*That's it, Caroline. That's just great. Lie here and turn yourself on, admiring your seducer instead of getting your butt out the door...*

Except, he hadn't seduced her.

He had taken her in his arms and kissed her. That was all he'd done. The choices afterward had been hers. She could have pushed him away. Slapped his face. She could even have let the kiss happen and then ended it and walked away. Nobody had forced her into his car, against that wall, into his bed...

Enough.

She breathed in, then slowly out. Inch by careful inch, she moved from beneath his arm. Waking him, having to face him again, was the last thing in the world she wanted.

If there was a morning protocol for what she was supposed to do now, she didn't know it, didn't want to know it.

*"Mmmf."*

Caroline froze. Waited. After what seemed forever, Lucas rolled onto his side, away from her.

She went into action, located her scattered clothes—shoes, dress, bra, little evening purse. She couldn't find her thong panties—her torn panties—and after a couple of minutes, she gave up looking.

Time to get out while she still could.

The gray light of dawn lit the rooms of the penthouse as she made her way downstairs. She had no memory of the place; all her attention had been on Lucas. Now, she saw that it was huge and handsome, furnished in light woods and glass. The elevator, small and elegant, stood at the end of the foyer.

Precious seconds flew while she figured out how to operate it. At last, she got it moving and as it dropped toward the lobby, she tried not to think about what had happened in this car a few hours ago.

Lucas, lifting her into him. His mouth, hungry on hers. Desire, welling hot and sweet within her.

The elevator gave a delicate bounce when it reached the lobby. The door slid open but not before Caroline got a clear look at herself in its mirrored surface.

What she saw made her cringe.

Smudged makeup. Tangled hair. Skinny gold heels and a dress that might as well have had *Guess What I Did Last Night* printed across it.

In a better world, the lobby would have been empty but this was the same world in which she'd already humiliated herself once. Now, it was time for Round Two.

A man in a blue blazer sat behind a desk. He looked up, saw her, smiled pleasantly and said, "Good morning, miss," as if women in her state stepped out of Lucas's private elevator all the time, which they undoubtedly did.

"Morning," she mumbled, but the embarrassment wasn't over, not yet, because—of course—there was a doorman and he said the same thing, just as pleasantly, and all Caroline could do was wish the marble floor would open and swallow her whole.

"Shall I hail a cab for you, miss?" the doorman said as he opened the door.

She said, "Yes, please," because even imagining getting into a subway car looking as she did at this hour of the morning made her feel sick.

"Thank you," she said, when a cab pulled to the curb. Was she supposed to tip the doorman or wasn't she? she wondered, and then she almost laughed because what did a question about tipping matter now? The fact was, she was in way over her head.

She gave the doorman a five-dollar bill, gave the cabbie her address and told herself that saying *I know how this looks but really, I'm not the kind of woman you think I am* would accomplish nothing. Either the cabbie wouldn't care or, if he did, then she was exactly the kind of woman he thought she was.

At least, she was that kind of woman, now.

She made it into her flat without bumping into anybody and then she locked the door, peeled off her dress—Dani's dress—kicked off her shoes—Dani's shoes—and went straight into the shower where not all the hot water nor all the soap in the world would have been enough to make her forget what she'd done.

If only she could forget the sex, the incredible sex, because it had been that. Incredible. Amazing. Fantastic. Or if she could remember it without feeling the awful guilt of having gone to bed with a man she didn't know.

But she couldn't. And, after a while, she just stopped trying.

Lucas awoke to a sound.

Faint. Distant. What…? The elevator. The purr of the motor.

He rolled over. Sat up. Saw that the space beside him was empty, that Dani's clothes were no longer scattered around the room.

She was gone.

He sank back against the pillows, folded his arms beneath his head. Well, that was a good thing. A very good thing. No need for forced early-morning conversation. No need to fend off offers to make coffee. No pretending that he loved having it with someone when he much preferred having it alone. No long, drawn-out goodbye.

He sat up again and swung his feet to the floor.

The only thing he ever wanted in the morning, besides black coffee and a shower, was sex. Wake-up sex, no frills, and women weren't into basics. None he'd ever encountered, anyway.

Besides, he thought as he headed for the bathroom, he had the feeling Dani Sinclair would have a bundle of morning-after recriminations. Not that she'd said "no" to anything last night—if she had, that would have been the end of it. But there'd been that innocence to her...

Ridiculous, of course. She had responded to him with unbelievable hunger, and that was another good thing. He wasn't into innocence or lack of experience—although he could see advantages to it.

To being the man who taught a woman what passion was all about.

He stepped into the shower, set the multiple sprays to produce a hot, needle-fine mist, bowed his head as the water sluiced on him and over him.

There'd been that moment when he'd teased Dani's dusty-pink nipples into tight little buds and she'd cried out as if something so simple was new. And later, when he'd parted her thighs, kissed her most intimate flesh, tasted her against his mouth...

Hell.

Lucas switched the water from hot to cold. Enough thinking about last night.

He had a long day ahead of him.

The day was not going well.

Lucas had sat through a morning meeting without hearing most of what was said. He'd canceled his lunch appointment. Now, he was at his desk, trying to answer a question that was as unanswerable as it was unimportant.

Why had Dani Sinclair run away?

What else could you call it when a woman spent the night in your bed and then disappeared without saying goodbye, without leaving a note, without leaving her phone number? Never mind seeing her again. Perhaps it was best that he not. But he had to get in touch with her. He hadn't paid her the thousand dollars for the work she'd done.

Hell. That wasn't going to come across well. Handing Dani money after they'd made love all night had an unpleasant connotation. Never mind. Business was business. He owed her money for the Rostov portion of the evening. What had happened after was not business; it had nothing to do with the fact that she'd translated for him.

And all of that brought him back to the initial question. Why had she vanished? He didn't like it. Women didn't walk out on him as Dani Sinclair had…and why did he keep thinking of her as if the name were one word instead of two? Because it didn't suit her? Ridiculous. Still, she'd said she didn't like the name, either. If she didn't, what name did she prefer?

Not that it mattered.

He had spent the night with her. Nothing more. So what if the name didn't suit her? So what if she'd walked out while he slept?

So what if he couldn't stop thinking about her, remembering the feel of her skin, the sweetness of her mouth…

"Mr. Vieira?"

Lucas rolled his eyes. Denise-Elise sounded pathetic even over the intercom.

"Yes?"

"Mr. Gordon's here to see you, sir."

Jack Gordon. Lucas's mouth thinned. He had no wish to see the man now but Gordon had done him a favor last night. Besides, Gordon would have Dani's address so that he could mail her the check he'd forgotten to give her.

"Tell him to come in."

Gordon smiled as he strolled through the door.

"Lucas. Well? How did things go?"

"Very well. In fact, I was going to call you to thank you and to ask for—"

"Was I right or was I right? I knew Dani would be perfect."

"Yes. She was. And I need her—"

"She's one amazing babe. Hot as well as smart. Some package, huh?"

Lucas wanted to get up from his chair, grab Gordon by the collar and toss him out. Instead, he mustered a polite smile.

"I'm busy this morning, Jack. So, thanks for recommending Ms. Sinclair. And please leave her address with my P.A."

"Dani's address? Why would you—" Jack Gordon smiled slyly. "Aha. The evening went that well, did it?"

Lucas narrowed his eyes. "I forgot to pay her."

Gordon raised his eyebrows. "Pay her?"

"The thousand I mentioned, although she deserves a bonus."

"A bonus?"

"What's her regular rate, do you know? I should have asked her but I—"

"But you got sidetracked." Gordon grinned and hitched a hip on the edge of Lucas's desk. "Yeah. Understandable. Her regular rate? Well, it ain't cheap."

"Just tell me what it is."

"For an evening? Ten K."

"Fine. Ten thou—" Lucas blinked. "What?"

"She's expensive. But you gotta know for yourself, she's worth every—"

A coldness seeped into Lucas's bones. "Nobody makes that kind of money translating."

"Translating?" Gordon laughed. "Sure, but Dani—"

"But Dani what?" Lucas's eyes flashed as he rose to his feet. "What does she do to earn that kind of money?"

Gordon stared at his boss. "She—she does—she does what she did for you last night. I mean, she did do something, uh, special for you, right?"

Lucas felt a stillness come over him. "Answer the question, Jack. What does Dani Sinclair do that earns her ten thousand dollars an evening?"

Jack Gordon's Adam's apple moved up and down in his throat. "She's—she's... You know. She's—she's an escort."

"An escort."

"Yeah. She, ah, she goes on dates with—with men. Like she did with you. And you have to admit, she's worth every—"

Lucas hit him. Hard. A right uppercut to the jaw. Gordon staggered, went down on one knee, his hand to his mouth. Lucas went around the desk, reached for him again…

And stopped.

An escort. A prostitute. He'd had sex with a woman who sold herself to any man who could afford her services.

A whore had spent the night in his bed.

His heart was beating hard and fast. His vision was blurred; he blinked to clear it. Gordon was still on one knee, face white, eyes wide with fear. Lucas felt his gut twist. Jack was a pig, but he'd let out his rage on the wrong person.

"Get up."

"Don't hit me again."

"Get up, damnit!"

"Lucas. Mr. Vieira. I should have told you."

"But you didn't."

"No. I thought—I thought maybe you wouldn't go for it, if you knew—"

"You thought, maybe it would be satisfying to make a fool of me."

Gordon winced, and Lucas knew he'd hit on the truth. He reached into a desk drawer, tossed Gordon a handful of tissues. Then he thrust a pad and pen across the desk. "Write down her address."

"Yeah, Sure. Look, I made a mistake, okay? I'm sorry. Really. I'm—"

"You're finished here, Gordon."

Jack Gordon's expression turned ugly.

"You think so? If I tell this story around—"

"Do it, and so help me God, you won't live long enough to enjoy it."

"You wouldn't…"

Lucas laughed. And Jack Gordon, hearing that laugh, looking into Lucas's eyes, knew that the game was lost.

Fridays were always the easiest day of Caroline's week.

During the school semester, she had a morning seminar. After that, she could go home and collapse. Now, with school over for the summer, the entire day was hers. Normally, that would have been great.

Not today.

Without something to do, memories of the night kept intruding. So when one of the waitresses at Dilly's Deli, where

Caroline had recently started working, called to ask if she could cover for her for a couple of hours, she said yes even though she already hated the place for its painfully clever menu, its spoiled but famous show business clientele, its ogling tourists.

By two o'clock, she regretted her decision. A family of tourists, five of them, had run up a bill of $120.00 and left her a two-dollar tip. A woman in booth four was still considering what to order after reading the menu for the past fifteen minutes. And the man in booth six, a puffed-up talk show host, had sent back his hamburger three different times.

"Your burger's up."

Caroline nodded to the middle-aged waitress who'd breezed by her, went through the swinging doors into the kitchen, retrieved the burger and took it to booth six.

At least you could take back a food order.

You couldn't take back behavior that made you want to die just thinking about it. Or, even worse, made you remember what it had felt like to be kissed and caressed as if nothing in the world mattered half as much as—

"Miss? Miss!"

Booth six. Caroline pasted a smile on her lips.

"Yes, sir?"

"Does the chef not understand the meaning of the word, 'rare'?"

Caroline looked at the burger. It was bleeding into its plate like an extra in a slasher movie. She picked up the plate, forced a smile, marched through the swinging doors into the kitchen and set the plate on the counter beside the grill.

"Not rare enough."

Caroline echoed the fry cook's sigh before she hurried back onto the serving floor just in time for the woman in booth three to make "check, please" motions with her fingers.

Caroline nodded, took her order pad from her pocket and

tallied the bill. It came to a lot but then, everything in this place was costly.

Not as costly as what she'd done last night.

Sex with a stranger. A sexy, gorgeous stranger.

Thinking about it made her cringe…except, except there was this tiny part of her that kept whispering, *Don't regret it. It was everything you ever dreamed and more.*

"Miss!"

*Oh God.* "Yes, sir?"

"Where is my hamburger?"

"Sir. You sent it back. The cook is—"

"I want it now, miss."

"But, sir—"

"Are you arguing with me, miss?"

"No. Certainly not. But—"

"Get the manager. Get him now! I am not going to be insulted by—"

It was the final straw. The job, the patrons… Enough. There were other restaurants, other jobs, and she had five hundred dollars coming to her. Last night, she'd thought how awful it would be to take that money but that was ridiculous. She had done what Dani had asked her to do, and that was what Dani would pay her for doing it.

Caroline tossed her order pad on the counter. Undid the tie of the frilly white apron all the waitresses wore and tossed it at the idiot in booth six.

"I beg your pardon," he sputtered.

Caroline flashed a smile. A real one, the first one since she'd awakened this morning.

"And well you should," she said sweetly.

And she left.

Should she call Dani, or just show up at her door? She'd never been to Dani's but she remembered the address. Just show up, she decided. Get the money Dani owed her and that would be that.

Dani's address turned out to be a brownstone on a trendy street in the sixties. Caroline raised her eyebrows. Maybe she only thought she'd remembered the address; maybe she had it wrong.

But when she rang the bell, it was Dani who opened the door.

"Caroline? What are you doing here?"

Caroline felt foolish. She was wearing jeans, a T-shirt and sneakers. Dani was wearing a scarlet dress cut to midthigh and knee-high, stiletto-heeled black leather boots. Her perfect face was perfectly made up; her brown hair seemed sexily windblown but any woman who'd ever spent two minutes struggling with hair that really was windblown would know a hairstylist had probably taken an hour to get it to look that way.

Caroline swallowed dryly. "I came to—to… You owe me money," she blurted.

"Oh. Oh, that's right, I do." Dani stepped back. "Well, don't just stand there. Come in. You can't stay long—I'm getting ready to go out."

"Go out where?" Caroline said, just to have something to say.

"Just out," Dani said briskly, heels tapping as she made her way across the clearly expensive floor of a designer-expensive living room. "Five hundred, right?" she said, opening her handbag.

Caroline nodded as she looked around her. She'd been in the apartments of a couple of other grad students. They all looked like hers: thrift shop furniture, dingy walls.

Dani's place was a palace.

"Wow," Caroline said softly.

Dani swung toward her, followed Caroline's gaze and smiled. "Like it?"

"It's beautiful."

Dani cocked her head. "You know," she said slowly, "you could have a place like this, if you wanted."

"Me?" Caroline laughed. "Right. By hitting the lottery."

Dani smiled again. "By working."

"Oh, sure."

"I'm serious, Caroline. I could, you know, get you started. Introduce you to some people, help you buy some clothes."

Caroline shook her head. "I don't understand. You mean, model?"

"Model?" Dani laughed. "Well, that's one way of considering it."

"Thanks, but I don't think—"

The doorbell pealed. Dani made a face. "I was *so* not expecting company this afternoon! Here." She held out five hundred-dollar bills. "Well, go on, take the money."

Caroline did. Hesitantly. Suddenly, accepting it seemed dead wrong. Her stomach gave a little jump.

"May I—may I use the bathroom?"

"Down the hall, on the right." Dani rolled her eyes as she *click-clicked* her way to the door. "Just be quick, okay? I told you, I have a date."

Caroline locked the bathroom door behind her. She felt hot and cold all at once. The money, the damned money had reminded her of everything all over again. Why had she come here? Why had she accepted the five hundred dollars? Well, she wouldn't. She'd give it back. She'd—

*Ohmygod!*

She could hear voices. Dani's. And a man's. Not just any man. The voice belonged to Lucas Vieira.

Quickly, she undid the lock. Stepped into the hall. Saw

Lucas, his tall, powerful body so familiar to her now. And Dani, facing him, hands on her hips, face tilted up.

"Of course I'm Dani Sinclair," she was saying. "And who the hell are you?"

"I am Lucas Vieira," Lucas growled. "And you are not Dani Sinclair."

"Don't be ridiculous! I should know who I—"

"Lucas?"

Caroline moved slowly down the hall. Lucas looked up. She saw the confusion in his eyes. "Dani?"

"Dani?" the real Dani said, and then she laughed. "I get it! You're the guy from last night. And you think that she, that Caroline, is me!"

Lucas's expression went from perplexed to confused. "What the hell is going on here?"

Caroline licked her lips. "I can explain. I'm really Caroline. Caroline Hamilton. See, Dani was supposed to—to be your translator—"

Lucas's mouth twisted. "My date, you mean," he said tonelessly. "The one Jack Gordon arranged."

"I don't know anybody named Jack Gordon. Dani arranged it. And yes, I was supposed to be your date."

"And you agreed."

"Well, yes. I didn't want to do it. I really, really didn't want to do it. But you have to understand, I needed the money."

"You needed the money." Lucas's gaze fell to the bills Caroline clutched in her hand, then rose to her face. *"Cristos,"* he growled, the word thick with disgust, "you needed the money."

Caroline drew herself up. "Five hundred dollars might not mean anything to you, but to me—"

Lucas swung toward Dani. "That's it? Gordon paid you your usual fee and all you gave her was five hundred dollars?"

"No one's paid me a dime yet," Dani said coolly. "All I've had out of this so far is more trouble than I really want."

"What usual fee? Who's Jack Gordon? What trouble?" Caroline came quickly forward, stopped inches from Lucas, whose anger was all but palpable. "Lucas." Her voice trembled. "Five hundred dollars is a lot of money. I needed it. And, for whatever it's worth, I've never done anything like that before."

She saw a stillness come over him, a coolness replace the rage.

"Haven't you?"

She shook her head. Pretend to be someone she wasn't? Of course not.

"No," she said emphatically, "never!"

"You want me to believe last night was your first time."

Caroline stiffened. "You act as if this was all my fault, but what about you? You were part of the game. You paid me to play a role."

The muscle in Lucas's jaw flickered. She was right. He'd paid her to pretend to be his lover. As for what had happened afterward...

That had been a role, too.

Going to bed with strangers was her profession. She was a call girl. A prostitute. A woman who sold herself to men. And he—he had thought, if only for a moment, that something special had happened between them.

Rage sent a flood of heat through his blood. He wanted to put his fist through the wall, to grab Caroline Hamilton and shake her like a rag doll.

Instead, he took out his checkbook and a gold pen, wrote two checks, tore both out and gave one to Dani Sinclair. She looked at it, then at him.

"Paid in full," he said coldly.

"Indeed, Mr. Vieira." She smiled. "Lucas."

"Stick with Mr. Vieira," he said, even more coldly, and held out the second check, to Caroline.

"What's that?" she asked in bewilderment.

"It's what I owe you for last night."

Heat shot into her face. "You don't owe me anything."

"Of course I do," he said impatiently. "I told Gordon I'd pay you a thousand dollars."

"No." Caroline shook her head; she took a quick step back, her eyes never leaving the check in his outstretched hand. "You don't owe me anything."

"Take the damned check!"

"I don't want it."

"I never renege on a deal." He shoved the check at her. "Take it."

"Lucas." Her voice trembled. "Whatever you're thinking—"

"You need the money," he said coldly, "remember? And I sure as hell had everything I needed from you."

She didn't move. All the color had drained from her face. Tears glittered in her eyes. Something inside him seemed to crack. He wanted to take her in his arms, kiss her until she stopped weeping.

*Cristos*, she was a damned fine actress.

But she would never make a fool of him again.

His hand closed around her wrist and he hauled her against him. He bent his head, took her mouth, kissed her hard enough to make her gasp. She raised her hand, balled it, hit his shoulder—and then her fist loosened, her fingers sought his cheek, spread over it and her lips softened under his, parted…

Lucas cursed.

Then he flung Caroline from him, let the check flutter to the floor and walked out.

# CHAPTER SIX

LUCAS knew he was in a dangerous frame of mind.

Caroline Hamilton had lied to him, not just about who she was but *what* she was. The knowledge that he had taken her to his bed made him furious.

He knew there was no point going back to his office. Making decisions, even dealing with people, would be a mistake when he was fighting to keep his temper under control.

He had to work off some of his energy, find a physical focal point for the adrenaline raging through him. Going to the gym would surely do it.

An hour later, he was sweaty, breathing hard—but his mood was still the same.

Okay, he thought grimly as he showered, okay, there was only one other way to deal with this. To hell with permitting one deceitful woman to take up residence in his head. If a horse threw you, you climbed right back on.

He had numbers in his BlackBerry, women he'd met, women who'd made it clear they were eager for him to call. Within minutes, he'd filled his weekend with enough variety to erase the memory of Caroline Hamilton forever.

He went home, shaved, changed, phoned a restaurant where it took a month to get a table and, of course, got one for eight o'clock and prepared to enjoy the hell out of a brunette who greeted him with a big smile.

Two hours later, he pleaded an early appointment the next morning, took her home and left her at her door.

"I had a wonderful time," she gushed, and he knew damned well it was a lie. He'd been the worst kind of company: silent, unsmiling, rushing her through a meal that normally would have taken three hours and then pretending he had no idea what she hinted at when she stepped close and turned her pretty face up to his.

"So did I," he said.

*Liar*, he thought…but not a liar anywhere near the equal of Caroline Hamilton.

He went back to his gym Saturday, played a couple of games of racquetball, lifted weights, traded the workout room for a run through Central Park. At night, instead of simply sending a check to a charity auction, he attended it with a redhead with an infectious smile and legs that went on forever. Afterward, he took her for a light supper because he knew it was the right thing to do but when she took his hand and said she lived nearby and the night was really young and it would be lovely if he came up for drinks, he pleaded another early appointment, delivered her to her door and left her there with a handshake.

*Merda*, a handshake!

He made himself a vow. He would do much better tomorrow, when he had a date to take a stunning Broadway actress to lunch.

If anything, he did worse.

"It isn't you," he said, when she asked him what was wrong, and before he could say, "it's me," she was on her feet and gone.

Enough.

He went home, packed, phoned his pilot, flew to Martha's Vineyard. A banker he knew had a weekend home on the beach; the guy and his wife were having a big party. They'd invited him but he'd declined.

"Turn up if you change your mind," the banker had said.

Well, he had definitely changed his mind.

He drank some excellent wine, ate a grilled-to-perfection lobster, got hit on by two women…and excused himself and went, alone, for a walk along the sand.

The day was not the kind chambers of commerce hope for. The sea was the color of pewter, the waves were high, the sky was bleak. All of that was fine.

It suited his mood.

Why in hell couldn't he stop thinking about Caroline? He despised her, despised what she was. So what if she was beautiful? He'd had the chance to get involved with several women equally beautiful in the past couple of days and he'd walked away from each one. He hadn't wanted to pretend interest in their conversations or smile at their jokes, and he sure as hell had not wanted to take one of them to bed.

And yet, he knew that if Caroline materialized in front of him at this moment, as willing and eager as she'd been the other night, he'd strip her of her clothes, take her in his arms, draw her down to the sand and bury himself inside her.

And she'd respond. No subterfuge, no games, no coy teasing.

"Damnit," he snarled, because it had *all* been subterfuge. She, and everything she'd done, had been an endless, ugly, practiced lie.

Turning him on, making all those little sounds, those whispers, driving him out of his mind with want and need…

They were the cornerstones of her profession. She traded sex for money.

And if there were moments it had seemed as if she'd never let a man do half the things he'd done to her that night, maybe that was her specialty. What had he heard it called, that blend of sex and innocence? The Madonna-whore thing. He'd never wanted those traits in a woman himself but then, he'd never been with a woman like Caroline before.

God knew, he would never be with one again.

The Elins of this world were more honest. They traded sex with powerful men for the tokens of that power. He wasn't a fool; he understood that. He'd always understood it. Jewels. Gifts. Being seen in the right places at the right times. It was what such women wanted and absolutely, that was more honest, wasn't it?

Wasn't it?

The sky went from gray to charcoal. Lightning flashed out over the Atlantic; rain beat down with a swift ferocity. He jogged back to the party, laughed along with everyone else at his soaked condition, took a taxi to the airport and got the hell out of Dodge.

Monday morning, things looked better.

He woke up feeling more like himself. His P.A. was back at her desk. His coffee tasted the way it was supposed to. Jack Gordon was history. Six months severance pay, no letter of recommendation.

Goodbye to the old, hello to the new. No question about it. Caroline Hamilton had become a meaningless memory.

He had meetings until noon, then a quick lunch at his desk. At one o'clock, in the middle of a complex telephone conversation with his attorney to tie up the final legalities of the Rostov deal, it all fell apart.

Nothing had changed. Why tell himself it had? That he'd filled the day with enough crap to keep six men busy was the sole reason he hadn't spent it staring out the window.

Gordon was a sneaky, ingratiating little worm. He'd deserved to be fired, but what penalty had Caroline paid? She had lied to him. The scene at Dani Sinclair's apartment, his show of anger, tossing that check at her, hadn't even come close to settling things.

And he had to do that. Settle things. Erase the memory of her lies. The only question was, how?

"Lucas?" his attorney was saying, "Lucas? Man, are you still there?"

Lucas took a breath. "Sorry. Yes, I'm here but something's come up." He paused. "Ted. If I needed an investigator…"

"I can recommend one." The lawyer rattled off a name and phone number, and then it was he who paused. "Can I help in any way?"

Lucas forced a chuckle. "No, no, it's nothing special."

The hell it wasn't.

He hung up the phone and got to his feet. The only way to put this behind him was to confront Caroline, tell her what he thought of her, tell her…

How should he know what he'd tell her? The right words would come when he saw her.

A couple of hours later, he had more information than he needed. All he'd wanted was Caroline's address. Now, he had her age: twenty-four. Her place of birth: some little town in upstate New York. Her education: an undergraduate degree in French. Now she was working toward a Master's degree in Russian and Slavic Studies.

The P.I. didn't come up with the rest of it, that she had an income on the side, but Lucas hadn't expected that he would. Caroline was clever. Her occupation, if you could call it that, would be carefully hidden.

Her address was no surprise at all.

She lived in one of those Manhattan neighborhoods that had gone from providing shelter for those who sweated to make enough to live on to providing it to those who had more money than they could ever need. It was home to hotshot young Wall Street traders who thought selling overvalued stocks entitled them to seven figure bonuses, and spoiled little rich girls whose parents funded their extravagant lifestyles while they played at working in the fashion business.

He'd been to a couple of dinner parties in Hell's Kitchen, so he knew what Caroline's place would be like.

An airy duplex in what had once been a tenement. A converted loft in what had once been a factory. Lots of pale wood, exposed brick, uncomfortable furniture and indecipherable art.

Expensive, but not a problem for a woman who was a student by day but had a source of income from an old but infinitely profitable profession.

Lucas almost laughed as he left his office.

Student by Day.

It sounded like the title of a bad movie. Only problem? It was real. And he, who had never paid for sex in his life, who had never been with a woman for any reason but mutual desire...

He had bought her services.

His laughter died.

"Goddamnit," he muttered, and a guy walking by on the street, even here in Manhattan where people never looked at each other, never showed a reaction, even here, the guy glanced at his face and detoured around him.

Traffic was a mess. Forget hailing a taxi. Walking was faster. And it kept him moving, which was what he needed right now.

Gradually, the streets changed, went from commercial to residential until, finally, he was in Caroline's neighborhood, then on her street.

It wasn't what he'd expected.

A handful of streets had not been converted from careworn to chic. This was one of them.

Overflowing trash cans lined the curb. Gang names and symbols adorned graffiti-filled walls. A fetid breeze sent bits of debris scattering along the sidewalk. All the buildings looked tired, Caroline's, in particular. It was a five-story pile of age-darkened red brick that seemed held together by a century's worth of grime.

A police car was parked in front of it.

Lucas felt his heart thump.

He knew some cops. They were, for the most part, good people. Still, thanks to his childhood in Rio, there were times when the sight of a police uniform or police car still made him uneasy.

This was one of those times.

And that was ridiculous. The cops were here. So what? It was not his problem.

The building's front door was not locked. His mouth thinned. Unlocked front doors were never a good idea but on streets like these, they were an invitation to trouble.

Not his problem, either.

The vestibule smelled bad. Dirt, cooking and something more pungent that was probably better not identified, hung thick in the air.

Again, not his concern.

There was another door ahead and, to his left, a panel of labeled call buttons. The one for apartment 3G read *C. Hamilton*.

At least Caroline had the good sense not to use her first name. Not that it mattered all that much. Using only a first initial was pretty much a giveaway that the name belonged to a woman.

He thought of the women he'd taken out over the weekend.

They all lived in buildings with security cameras, locks and what looked like retired wrestlers as doormen.

So what? Caroline's security—or the lack of it—came under that same not-my-problem heading, as did the fact that the interior door yawned onto a dim hall.

How she lived meant nothing to him.

It just ticked him off that an intelligent woman—and she was smart, he had to give her that—would live in a place like this. It certainly couldn't be because of money, not when she made her living as she did.

Lucas frowned.

Then, why had she let him pay her only a thousand dollars for that night in his bed? God only knew what being with her should have cost him. He'd never put a price on such things but if he had—if he had...

Lucas spat out a word that was as ugly in Portuguese as it would have been in English. Who gave a damn? Not him.

He took the sagging stairs and paused on the third-floor landing. Apartment 3G was directly ahead. That feeling of unease, an icy clenching in his gut, swept through him again.

Something was definitely wrong.

The police car at the curb. The unnatural quiet of the old building, broken now by the barely imperceptible *snick* of the door to the apartment adjoining Caroline's opening an inch, then quickly closing again.

He moved forward fast, pressed his hand, flat, against her buzzer, then hammered his fist against the door.

"Caroline?" He grasped the knob, rattled it. "Damnit, Caroline—"

The door swung open. Caroline stood before him, wearing sweats, no makeup, her face pale, eyes reddened, her hair damp and wild on her shoulders.

"Mother of God," he said hoarsely, "*querida*, what is it?"

"Lucas," she said, "Lucas…"

Every logical thought, all the rage, all the bitter desire for payback, flew out of his head. He opened his arms and she flew into them.

He gathered her to his heart, held her close, whispered soothing words to her in Portuguese. She was trembling; he thought of a puppy he'd once found in an alley in Rio, how it had whimpered and trembled, how he had held it in his arms until it was silent and still…

"Caroline. Sweetheart. *Que aconteceu?* What happened?"

"A man," she said. "A man…"

"Excuse me, sir."

Lucas swept her behind him at the sound of the male voice. Every muscle in his body went on alert—but the source of the voice was a uniformed police officer, emerging from a doorway to the left. A second, shorter officer stood just behind him.

The cops from the patrol car.

His blood became a river of ice.

"What happened here?" he demanded.

The first officer took a step forward.

"Sir? Please identify yourself."

What he wanted to do was sweep Caroline into his arms and take her from this place, to turn back the clock so that it was still Thursday night and she was safe in his bed.

"Sir?"

Lucas nodded as he curved his arm around Caroline and drew her to his side.

"I am Lucas Vieira. And I asked you a question."

"Are you a friend of Ms. Hamilton's, Mr. Vieira?"

Caroline turned against him and buried her face in his shoulder. Lucas nodded again.

"I am a very good friend of Ms. Hamilton's, Officer."

"And you're here because…?"

"I've answered all the questions I intend to answer until you tell me what happened."

"Someone broke into Ms. Hamilton's apartment."

The other policeman stepped aside, revealing what had been a window and was now an empty frame for the rusted iron fire escape that clung to the building's exterior wall.

Glass littered the linoleum floor.

Lucas's vision reddened, narrowed until he could see only the broken window. He felt rage like none he had ever known before.

"Caroline." He clasped her shoulders and looked at her pale face. "Tell me who did this."

She shook her head. "I never saw the man before."

"What did he do to you?" She didn't answer and he knew he was nearer the total loss of the civilized man he was supposed to have become than he had ever been in his entire life. "Sweetheart. *Querida*, did he hurt you?"

She drew a long, tremulous breath.

"No."

"Are you sure? Because if he did—"

"He didn't—he didn't touch me. I screamed and—and—"

Her breath hitched. Her face was turned up to his; her lips were parted. He fought back the desire to gather her against him and kiss away the terror in her eyes.

"I was—I was just coming out of the shower. I thought I heard something break. Glass, I thought. In the kitchen."

She nodded toward a wall where a refrigerator that would have looked at home in one of the better Rio *favelas* leaned drunkenly against an ancient stove.

"So—so I came out of the bathroom. I wasn't expecting to see anything but broken glass on the floor, you know, something the cat knocked over, and—"

"The cat," Lucas said, because he had to grab on to

something simple or the fury inside him inside him would surely explode.

"Yes. My cat. Well, he's my cat now. I mean, I found him yesterday. Sunday, when I went down to get the paper, just sitting huddled by the stoop, and—"

"Caroline." Lucas cleared his throat. "What happened?"

"I saw the broken glass on the floor. And—and I saw the man. He was coming through the window. I screamed. And it must have been a really loud scream because Mr. Witkin, who lives next door, he banged on the wall the way he does if I play my CDs too loud except I don't, I don't ever play them loud at all—"

She began to weep. Soundlessly, shoulders shaking, which somehow turned Lucas's hot rage to icy fear. He gathered her into his arms again and held her close.

"The intruder took off. Ms. Hamilton phoned 911," the taller cop said.

"The police came right away," Caroline whispered.

Lucas looked at the two officers. "Thank you," he said, and meant it. "Thank you for everything."

Both of them nodded.

"Yeah. We just wish we could have caught the bas—the guy."

Lucas would have preferred catching the bastard himself, but he thought it best not to say so.

"There's been a rash of break-ins on this street the last couple of weeks," the smaller policeman said. "Same M.O. Guy breaks a window, comes in, takes whatever isn't nailed down…"

"Lately," the other cop said, "he's upped the ante." His eyes darted to Caroline, who was trembling in Lucas's arms. "He's been targeting apartments where women live alone, you know…" He paused; clearly, there was more, but he wasn't about to say it.

"The lady better get that window fixed," the smaller officer said. "Have a grill put in. Should have had one there all along. Windows that lead out to fire escapes are bad news."

"Yes," Lucas said, half-amazed he could say anything at all. He cleared his throat. "Are you finished speaking with Ms. Hamilton?"

The cops nodded. "We might need to get in touch with her again, but for now—"

Lucas let go of Caroline, got out his black leather business card holder and a pen, scrawled his home address on the back of a card and handed it over.

"You can reach Ms. Hamilton at that address," he said, putting his arm around her again, "should you need her."

"No," Caroline said quickly. "You can reach me right here. I'll get the window fixed and—"

"That is incorrect. Ms Hamilton will be staying with me."

"Lucas." Caroline looked up at him, calmer now, her voice steadier though she was still trembling. "I couldn't possibly—"

"Let me see you out, Officers," Lucas said politely, as if there were a formal hallway before them rather than a door.

He held out his hand; both men shook it. He watched them start down the stairs. Then he closed the door, took a breath and swung toward Caroline, all the while telling himself to be calm. He knew she was going to argue about going with him and that he would tolerate no argument, and he knew, too, that the last thing she needed was to have him snap at her…

Or have him take her in his arms and kiss her until color returned to her face.

And what kind of nonsense was that? He'd come here for closure. Just because he'd found not a brittle, defiant Caroline but a fragile one, just because some faceless monster had come within inches of doing God only knew what to her…

None of that changed anything.

Of course, it didn't.

He didn't feel any differently toward her. He was just doing what any decent man would when he saw a woman in a difficult situation.

There was nothing like regaining perspective.

"All right," he said evenly. "Here's what is going to happen. You'll pack a few things, only what you think you'll need immediately."

"Thank you for your concern. It's very kind, but—"

"My driver will pick up the rest later."

Caroline stood a little straighter. "You're not listening. I appreciate your offer, but—"

"It isn't an offer. It's what you're going to do."

She looked at him. The color was coming back into her face. It hadn't taken his kisses to get it there, after all.

"If I decide to leave here," she said carefully, "I'll stay with a friend."

A muscle knotted in his jaw. "What friend?"

"I don't know. Someone. It isn't your problem."

She was right. Nothing about her was his problem. Wasn't that what he'd been telling himself for the past hour?

"What friend?" he heard himself say again.

"I just told you—"

"Jack Gordon?"

"I already told you, I don't know any Jack Gordon."

Lucas looked at her. "Dani Sinclair, then. Will you stay with her?"

Caroline's eyes flashed. "Dani and I are in the same graduate program. She's not a friend."

No, he thought coldly. The Sinclair woman was a business associate… But this wasn't the time for that.

"So, what friend will you stay with?"

"Goodbye, Lucas."

"Goodbye?" He moved toward her even as he asked himself what in hell he was doing. "A few minutes ago, you were so glad to see me that you threw yourself into my arms."

"A few minutes ago, the only people I'd seen today were a burglar and two cops." She stood even straighter, as if her spine had turned into steel. "I'd have thrown myself at Bozo the Clown, if he'd walked through that door."

"Such a compliment, *querida*. I am flattered."

She folded her arms; he folded his. It occurred to him that they probably resembled a pair of fighters, squaring off at a weigh-in.

"Once again," she said, "thank you. But—"

"You are coming with me, Caroline." He smiled grimly. "One way or another."

"Oh, for heaven's sake!" She stalked toward him, chin lifted, eyes defiant, more beautiful than any woman had a right to be, and jabbed a finger into the center of his chest. "Listen to me, Mr. Vieira. I make my own decisions. Understand? And I am not going anywhere with you!"

"Your choice," he said calmly. "On your own two feet, or slung over my shoulder."

She stared at him, her breasts rising and falling in the quick measure of her breath. Good, he thought. At least he had chased her fear away.

"You," she said coldly, "have not heard anything until you've heard me scream."

"And you," he said, just as coldly, "have not heard anything until you've heard me explain to your Mr. Sitkin—"

"Witkin," she said, through her teeth.

"Until you've heard me explain to Mr. Witkin why I, as your *nuivo*, cannot possibly—"

"My what?"

"Your fiancé, *querida*," Lucas purred. "I'm sure Mr. Witkin will be most sympathetic after I explain that what happened to you a little while ago has left you somewhat unstable and that I can use his help opening doors for us as I carry you downstairs so I can put you in my car and take you to my physician's office."

"He'd never fall for that!"

Lucas flashed a smile. "Want to bet?"

"Damn you, Lucas Vieira!"

"Damn me, indeed. But that's how it's going to be. You're coming with me, Caroline. Your only choice is how."

She glared at him. Despite everything, he wanted to laugh. Such fire in her. Such defiance.

"Very well," she said through gritted teeth. "I'll do this. For one night. But I warn you, I am not interested in having you—in letting you—"

"In letting me what?" he said, and he reached for her, took her in his arms and kissed her the way he'd wanted to kiss her ever since he'd come through the door.

She stiffened. Then she gave a little sigh, leaned into him, kissed him back...

"Yeow!"

Sharp, hot knives dug into Lucas's leg. He jumped back, looked down, saw an emaciated thing the size of a Cocker Spaniel attached to his leg.

Caroline looked down, too... And laughed.

"Oh my goodness! Oliver!"

She bent, snatched the creature into her arms and stood up. An enormous, bony, painfully ugly cat glared wildly at him through malevolent yellow eyes.

"*Merda,*" he said, "what is that?"

"It's Oliver," Caroline crooned, burying her face in the animal's fur. "My cat." The cat turned its big head toward her, purred and butted its jaw against hers. "Poor baby. He's terrified."

Rabid, seemed more like it. No blood, Lucas thought,

dragging up his cuff and checking, but what did that matter when what had to be the most mangy creature in cat-dom attacked you?

"Oliver," he said flatly, as it all fell into place. "The cat you found yesterday?"

"In the street. Yes. Dirty. Half-starved. Scared to death of everything."

"It's still dirty," Lucas said, narrowing his eyes.

"He. Oliver is a he. And he's not dirty anymore. I gave him a bath last night." Caroline nuzzled the animal again. "He just has a splotchy coat, that's all."

"He doesn't look scared, either. Not scared enough to want to let me live."

Carolyn giggled. It was so unexpected, all things considered, and such a lovely sound that he had a difficult time not smiling.

"He's wary around people, that's all." The cat made a delicate sound, a meow that should have come from a purebred kitten instead of the bedraggled beast in Caroline's arms. "But not me, because I saved him."

"How fortunate for you both."

"You may find this amusing but I promise you, it isn't. I'm Oliver's person. The one he's always going to love. He must have thought were trying to hurt me."

Lucas nodded. "And, of course, you're not going to want to leave him here." The look on Caroline's face was all the answer he needed. "Okay," he said briskly, and took out his cell phone. "I'll make a couple of calls. The first to my driver, so he can pick us up. The second to a guy I know on the board at the ASPCA—"

"What?"

"The American Society for the Protection of An—"

"I know what the initials mean but if you think I'm going

to give Oliver to a place that will put him in a cage and—and destroy him—"

"They'll put him in a foster home," Lucas said, though he couldn't imagine anyone insane enough to give shelter to the creature. "And he won't be destroyed."

Caroline narrowed her eyes. "Oliver goes with me."

"Caroline. Be sensible. That cat—"

"He goes with me or I stay put."

"Damnit, woman—"

"And why did you come here today, anyway?" Her chin rose. "That last time I saw you, in Dani's apartment, was more than enough for me."

"That has nothing to do with this."

"It has everything to do with it! You acted as if—as if I were dirt under your feet and now, here you are, playing at being a knight come to rescue a damsel in distress."

"Look, maybe I overreacted that last time, okay?" Hell, maybe he had. He'd hired Caroline to do a job. And she'd done it well. If anyone were to blame for what had happened, it was Jack Gordon for not telling him, up-front, that Caroline was—that she was more than a translator.

And why was he letting her take this conversation off-track?

"Very well," he said brusquely. "You can bring the cat. Go on, pack what you need. I'm tired of wasting time."

"Good. So am I. And just so you know, if you'd tried to drag me out of here, if you'd lied to Mr. Witkin, I'd have screamed so loud the cops would have come back!"

They glared at each other. Then Caroline thrust the cat at him.

"Here. Well, go on. Take him. I can't pack and hold Oliver at the same time!"

The skinny, writhing denizen of hell landed on his chest and inserted all its claws into his suit jacket. Lucas looked at the cat. The cat looked at him. A demonic sound vibrated in its throat.

One last attempt at sanity, Lucas thought, and made a wild grab at anything that seemed reasonable.

"I'm not sure pets are permitted in my building."

Caroline laughed.

He couldn't blame her.

She knew, as well as he, that whether pets were permitted or not would never matter to him. If he wanted to house a Martian with two heads and six tentacles and Martians were not allowed in his building, he would simply get himself a Martian and march it straight through the lobby.

The thing was, he didn't understand why people had pets. Get attached to something, it dies on you. Or walks away. Even if it didn't, anything you developed affection for demanded a lot of time and care and he could not imagine what it would give in return.

Still, this wasn't the time to explain his philosophy. Besides, why would he have to explain anything about himself to anyone?

"Just get on with it," he snapped.

Caroline tossed her head and walked into the bedroom. Lucas held the cat in one arm. That sound emerged from its throat again.

"Do not push your luck, cat," he said in a low voice.

Then he called his driver, arranged for him to meet them at the curb. As he concluded the call, Caroline emerged from the bedroom clutching an overflowing tote bag in the curve of one arm and a potted plant in the other.

"It's a fern," she said coldly, before he could say anything. "And, yes, I found it on the street, too, and yes, it's coming with me. It needs care."

What it needed, Lucas thought, was a vial of bleach and a quick burial.

She strode past him, arms overflowing, and somehow managed to free a hand and open the door.

"I know it's hard for you to understand," she said over her shoulder, "but I don't believe in letting living things suffer."

Lucas, following after her as the cat tried to claw its way to freedom through his suit jacket, through his shirt and, *Deus*, through his flesh, could only wonder if that philosophy might yet apply to him.

# CHAPTER SEVEN

A THIRTY-TWO million dollar penthouse. A place that could have made the pages of *Architectural Digest*, if Lucas had not been so protective of his privacy.

On the walls, an eclectic mix of Japanese woodcuts, Mark Rothko paintings and Lucas's latest find, a moody and magnificent Edward Hopper oil.

On the floors, antique Tabriz carpets over Brazilian rosewood.

In the twelve light-filled rooms, soaring ceilings, pale cherry furniture, low white silk sofas and fresh flowers massed in beautiful Steuben vases and bowls.

Now, two new pieces had been added. The fern that looked like a Pleistocene leftover was—well, it was somewhere in the guest suite. Caroline had lugged it up the stairs after she had Oliver settled in. Lucas had offered to carry it but she'd refused him.

"I'm perfectly capable of doing it myself," she'd said coolly.

Now, she and the fern were out of sight.

A bright red cat litter pan was not. It stood in the elegant downstairs lavatory. It was a hooded pan, for sure, but there was no disguising its purpose, especially now, Lucas thought grimly, as he made the mistake of glancing toward the lavatory just in time to see the somewhat battered head of the cat poke out the hole in the pan's domed cover.

The cat and Lucas made eye contact.

The cat hissed. Its ears, what there were of them, folded back.

"The same to you, pal," Lucas muttered, and kept going.

That there was a dying fern in his home seemed improbable. That there was a litter pan seemed impossible. That he was the person who'd purchased it seemed beyond logic, but it had been that or have Caroline hand him the cat again after they'd settled in the backseat of his limo, the fern on the floor, the cat once again in her arms.

"We'll have to make a stop," she'd said. "Oliver will need some things."

Lucas had decided there was nothing to be gained by pointing out that what Oliver needed was a personality transplant.

"A pet shop. Or a drugstore will do."

Lucas had leaned forward. "Stop at the Duane Reade on the next block, please, James," he'd said.

His driver had complied, pulling to the curb in front of the all-purpose pharmacy.

And Caroline had held out the cat.

The cat had looked at Lucas and hummed. Lucas narrowed his eyes, hoped the cat was half as good at reading minds as it was at drawing blood and reached for the door handle instead.

"I'll go in," he'd said coldly. "Just tell me what you need."

It was the first time he'd ever gone up and down the aisles of a Duane Reed. Of any store, other than Saks or Tiffany's or Barney's, for that matter, in a very, very long time.

It was also the first time he'd stood in a queue of people waiting to pay for their purchases. It was not an experience he was eager to repeat, especially not while he balanced two litter pans, two covers, half a dozen cans of something called Daintee Deelites, a bag of Kitty Krunchies, and two plastic things euphemistically called litter scoops.

When he'd finally emerged from the store, his driver sprang from the car, went to the rear and opened the trunk. Caroline, who'd watched him as he approached, put down her window.

"Where's the litter?"

The litter.

His driver had coughed. Lucas had glared. And if The Cat from Hell could have flashed a feline smile, he was sure that it would have done so.

"Shall I go, sir?" his driver had asked.

But Lucas had already turned away and marched back to the store. This time, at least, he knew the correct aisle but the wait to pay was just as long.

He'd been tempted to ask Caroline if the cat would like to make a stop at Zabar's for smoked salmon, but he had the uneasy feeling she might have said yes.

Now, a handful of hours later, he stood at the wall of glass in his living room, watching the lights come on in Central Park and wondering how he, a man who had set out to confront a woman who had lied to him, could have ended up in this situation.

His orderly, well-planned life was in total disarray. How else to describe it?

There was a cat peeing, or worse, in his bathroom. A dead plant sucking up oxygen in his guest suite. The second litter pan was also there, which explained why Caroline had ordered him to purchase two.

*I'd confine Oliver to my rooms with me,* she'd said, *but he's accustomed to the streets. He might not take well to confinement behind a closed door.*

Evidently not.

There was also a pair of Mikasa stoneware soup bowls on the Italian tile kitchen floor, one filled with the contents of a can of Daintee Deelites—which, it turned out, looked like tuna and smelled like nothing Lucas ever wanted to smell again—and the other filled with water.

"Soup bowls?" Lucas had said, and Caroline had given him a look he was coming to know and said yes, soup bowls, because he had neglected to buy dishes for Oliver.

He'd opened his mouth to tell her she had neglected to request them, but what was the point? Then she'd stroked her hand slowly, slowly down the cat's back but the cat had ignored her in favor of burying its face in the bowl of Daintee Deelites, and Lucas had thought what a damned fool the animal was, choosing food over the soft touch of Caroline's hand.

That was when she'd asked him where she was to stay.

He'd looked at the cat, looked at her and come within a heartbeat of saying, *Where do you think you're going to stay? In my bed, damnit, and get yourself there right now.*

But he hadn't. Why would he? The last place he'd ever want her again was in his bed.

She was a liar and a cheat. She was more than that, and just because she lived on the edge of poverty, just because she'd taken in a dying plant and a starving cat when dozens, maybe hundreds of New Yorkers had walked by and probably never even noticed the animal, didn't change a thing.

It couldn't.

She was what she was, who she was, and he could never accept that. Not that he had to, any more than he had to like the fact that she was here, plant, cat and all, messing up his life.

Lucas turned from the window, walked mindlessly through the living room, turning on lamps and chandeliers until the huge space seemed to blaze with man-made fire. Then he stood still, tilted back his head and stared at the ceiling.

"Hell," he muttered, and he went into his study, closed the door and sank into a leather armchair.

In the dark.

The truth was—and truth mattered, if he was going to be such a damned stickler about honesty—the truth was that he was the only one to blame for this mess.

Caroline was in his life because he'd hired her to play a part. She was in his home because he'd insisted on it. What kind of man would leave a woman, any woman, in a place with doors that you couldn't lock and an intruder who might decide to pay another visit?

Sure, he'd gone to her apartment to confront her but could he have done that after she'd flown into his arms, trembling, saying his name as if it were all that could keep her safe?

Lucas rose to his feet, tucked his hands into his trouser pockets and paced the room.

He had done the right thing. The only thing. But he had his feet on the ground. He wasn't going to get drawn in any deeper. He knew exactly how to handle things when life threatened to turn you inside out. Take a logical approach. Determine the problem, find the solution.

He was good at that.

Better than good.

It was why he had come so far.

Even these few moments of rational thought had been enough to clarify the situation.

He knew half a dozen top Realtors. One phone call, and his problem would be solved. Caroline would probably claim she couldn't afford whatever a Realtor found and he wouldn't argue, wouldn't ask what a woman who earned her living selling herself did with all her money...

*Five hundred dollars is a lot of money. I needed it. And, for whatever it's worth, I've never done anything like that before.*

He could hear her saying those words in his head. Maybe it was true. Maybe that night she'd spent with him really had been the first time she'd put a price on sex…

Lucas scowled. What did it matter? Her finances were her business. He didn't want to know anything about them, or her. He would simply pay a couple of months rent in advance, hell, he'd pay for the year, and that would be that.

And if he never managed that confrontation, so what? Someday, he'd look back on this entire thing and laugh. Lucas Vieira, taken in by an innocent girl who'd turned out not to be innocent at all.

Sure he would. He'd laugh.

His mouth twisted.

And if he didn't laugh, that was okay, too. He would get past this. He was a man, not a boy. He would move on.

Lucas took his telephone directory from his desk, leafed through it, chose a Realtor he'd dealt with in the past. It was late, but so what?. Being able to call someone at virtually any hour was one of the perks of having power and money.

The call was brief. He wanted an apartment for a friend. In the fifties. On Madison or Park, or just off those streets. One bedroom. A building with a doorman, of course, as if there were any other kind in this neighborhood. And a security system. Yes. Cameras, video, whatever was current. Price didn't matter.

He hung up and felt relieved.

Why mention it to Caroline until it was a done deal? he decided, and after a few minutes, he stood up and paced the room some more.

Time dragged by.

He listened for any sounds from upstairs. Nothing. There was a woman in his home and he might as well have been alone.

Which was fine.

He liked it that way.

Still, Caroline was here. Didn't she intend to come down and say something? Say anything? What about eating? He was hungry; he hadn't had a thing except coffee and that was hours ago. She had to be hungry, too.

Was she waiting for an invitation?

Maybe so. Maybe she expected him to knock on her door and invite her to join him for dinner.

He could take her out to dinner, instead.

There was a quiet little restaurant a couple of blocks away. It was small. Intimate. Candles on the tables. The kind of place where the owner came by and told you what was on the night's menu. He'd only been there once. With Elin, but Elin hadn't liked it.

"I never heard of this place," she'd said with faint but perceptible disdain. "And I don't see a person I know."

He suspected Caroline wouldn't say anything remotely like that. If her lover took her to a dimly lit restaurant, her lover's face would be the only one that interested her...

Lucas snorted. Who cared what she would say or do? Besides, he thought coldly, the word "lover" didn't have much meaning in her life. She would say or do whatever a man wanted her to say or do. That was what she'd done the other night, wasn't it? Starting in the hotel lobby, going right through dinner...

And ending in his bed.

"Hell!"

How many times was he going to go over this nonsense? Enough was enough, he thought, and strode toward the kitchen. Whether she ate or not, what she did or didn't do, wasn't his business. Right now, his business was to put food in his empty belly.

This was his housekeeper's regular day off. No problem.

There were always neatly marked packets of ready-to-heat things in the freezer, eggs and bacon in the refrigerator and, better still, take-out menus in the kitchen desk drawer.

Lucas reached the kitchen, opened the fridge, took out a bottle of Corona…

The cat came barreling out of the darkness and shot between his legs. There was no telling which of them was the more startled—but Lucas was the only one holding a glass bottle. It slid from his grasp and shattered against the tile floor.

He jumped back.

Too late.

The cold beer splashed over his shoes and trouser cuffs, splattered the stainless steel door of the refrigerator and the pristine ivory walls. Lucas stared at the mess and then he raised his arms, hands knotted into fists and wagged them at the ceiling.

"That's it," he shouted. "I've had enough. More than enough!"

"What happened?"

The kitchen lights came on. He swung around and saw Caroline in the doorway. She was still wearing the baggy sweats, her hair was flattened on one side, her eyes were bleary. One look, and he knew she'd been asleep.

Asleep while his life got turned upside down. While he tiptoed around his own home like a stranger, while he dealt with a psychotic cat, while he wasted time trying to figure out how an ordinary, perfectly normal man could have got himself into a situation like this.

She didn't look beautiful anymore, she looked like a woman who needed to comb her hair and put on makeup and some decent clothes, and how could that make him want to haul her into his arms and kiss her until she was breathless?

Her gaze flew to the broken glass, then to his face.

"Oh. Did Oliver…?" She swallowed. "Lucas. It isn't his fault. I told you, he's terrified of—"

"Is that the only living creature you give a damn about? Oliver?"

She was pale. Frightened. He could see it in her eyes but he didn't care. He was frightened, too. Of going crazy, because that was what was surely happening to him, he was going freaking crazy, trying to make sense out of what was happening to his carefully organized life.

"Please. Tell me what happ—"

"I'll tell you what happened," he snarled, because anger was an emotion he understood and he sure as hell didn't understand much else, not anymore. He walked quickly toward her, shoes crunching over glass, and stopped an inch away. "I hired you to translate for me and instead, you—you—"

"I what?" she said in bewilderment.

"Instead, you—you…" Lucas clasped her shoulders. "Damnit, Caroline," he growled, and he pulled her into his arms and kissed her.

Kissed her hard. Deep. Kissed her again and again, clasping her face between his big hands, thrusting his tongue between her lips, forcing his kisses on her…

Until he realized that he wasn't.

She was kissing him back.

Her lips were parted to his. Her hands were knotted in his shirt. She was standing on tiptoe, soft, exciting little moans coming from her throat.

"Lucas," she whispered against his mouth, "Lucas…"

Lucas groaned, cupped her bottom, lifted her into the hard urgency of his body. She gasped and moved against him.

"We can't do this," she whispered.

"We can. We have to."

"We can't. It's wrong…"

"Then tell me to stop, *querida*. Say it, and I'll let you go."

"Stop," she said, but her body was pressed to his, her mouth was warm and open against his mouth.

Lucas caught her wrists.

"I want you. I want you more than I've ever wanted a woman. And it has to be the same for you, do you understand? You have to want me. Me. Lucas Vieira. No games. No masquerade. No pretense. Because if that isn't how it is for you—"

"That's exactly how it is," she said, and he swung her into his arms, and carried her up the stairs, to his bedroom. To his bed.

His hands, his body, were shaking.

He wanted to take her as he should have taken her that very first time they'd been together.

But he couldn't wait. He couldn't, and there was no sense in wondering why he was so out of control because it wouldn't change anything. His need, his hunger, were almost unbearable.

Still, he used the last of that control to try to make her understand what was going to happen.

"Listen to me," he said roughly. "I want to make slow love to you. I want to touch you until you beg me for release." His hand slid under her sweatshirt; he cupped her breast, stroked her nipple and she cried out and arched toward him. "But I can't. Not now. Do you understand? I need you too badly. This time. This way. No holding back, no finesse, no—"

"Damnit," Caroline said, "damnit, Lucas…"

She pushed his hand away. Sat up. Yanked her sweatshirt over her head. Pulled off her sweatpants.

She was wearing a white cotton bra. White cotton panties. Nothing exotic, nothing silk, nothing lace, just her, just Caroline, and it was all he'd ever wanted.

He told her, in Portuguese, how beautiful she was. How he

hungered for her, and as he did, he stripped off his clothes, then the last of hers.

She lay back. Gave herself up to him. His mouth. His hands. His body. Her eyes grew dark, her breathing quickened, his name sighed from her lips as his sweat-slicked skin met hers and the broad head of his swollen penis brushed against her.

"Caroline," he said, the one word hot and urgent, and he thrust into her.

Caroline cried out. Not with pain, though he was deep inside her, so deep that, for a heart-stopping moment, she wondered if she could take all of him in.

Her cry was one of ecstasy. Of fulfillment. Of knowing that this, only this, was what she had been created for. Of knowing that she wanted him, wanted him, wanted him. Her muscles quivered, her body accepted the exquisite intrusion.

"Lucas," she sobbed, "oh, Lucas…"

Tears slipped down her cheeks.

He kissed them away. Kissed her mouth. And then he began to possess her, to drive her toward that place he, only he, had taken her before.

His strokes were hard. Demanding. Possessive. She loved it, loved the sense of being his, of belonging to him, of being claimed by him.

And then she stopped thinking.

The world spun. Her vision dimmed. Caroline cried out, Lucas threw back his head and groaned, and they flew over the edge of the universe, together.

# CHAPTER EIGHT

THEY lay sprawled across the big bed, breathing hard, skin salt-slicked, Lucas's powerful body over Caroline's.

Slowly, the world righted itself.

She sighed, turned her head, kissed his shoulder. He murmured something she couldn't understand but that was all right because it was enough to understand this. That she was with him, lying with him, feeling the race of his heart against hers, the weight of his muscled strength bearing her down into the softness of the cool linen sheets.

He kissed her temple. Stroked one big hand the length of her side, his thumb sliding over her nipple, then over the curve of her hip.

"I'm too heavy for you," he murmured, and she responded by putting her hand at the base of his spine. The feel of him against her, warm and hard and male, was too wonderful. She didn't want him to move, didn't want either of them to move, not in this lifetime or any other.

Still, after another couple of minutes, he lifted his head, brushed his lips over hers and rolled onto his side.

"No," she whispered, and he slid his arm under her shoulders and drew her close against him.

"I'm not going anywhere," he said softly, and she turned toward him and pressed her face against him, her nose at the junction of his shoulder and his arm. She loved the smell of him there, earthy and masculine.

"That was," he said, "that was—"

"Yes," she said. "It certainly was."

He laughed softly and pressed a kiss to her tangled hair.

"I'm just sorry I was so fast, but—"

"You were perfect."

"We were perfect," he said. "Perfect together."

Her heart did a little dance step. She tilted her head and looked into his face. Such a beautiful, sexy face. She wanted to tell him that but she had the feeling he was not a man who'd want to be referred to as "beautiful."

She smiled. He smiled back at her, and kissed her with such tenderness that her throat constricted.

*"Querida?"* His tone softened. "Seriously. Are you sure you're all right?"

"Yes."

"Because…I know, truly, it was fast—"

"Lucas. It was wonderful. It was everything I—I—"

He rolled again so that now he was on his belly, one arm lying across her, his eyes intent on hers.

"It was everything you what?"

Caroline felt her face heat. "It was everything I've dreamed of since—since—"

"Since that night."

She nodded. "Yes."

He said nothing for a long minute. Then he traced the outline of her mouth with the tip of his index finger.

"Then why did you run away from me?"

"I didn't run. I left."

"You ran, Caroline. In the middle of the night. Without leaving me your phone number. Without leaving me anything but memories I couldn't erase."

She put her hand to his cheek, felt the roughness of the end-of-day stubble. He turned his face and kissed her palm.

"I took my memories with me," she said softly.

That made him smile. "Yeah?"

She loved that simple "yeah," filled with arrogance though it was. She didn't like arrogant men; her mother might have been a fool for the type, but she wasn't.

But Lucas was different.

His arrogance was part of him. It wasn't an act meant to impress others, it was raw self-confidence, very male, very appealing.

Incredibly sexy.

"You're not going to run away this time."

She looked into his eyes. They were as dark as she'd ever seen them, and hot with something that made her breath quicken. His body was stirring against hers.

Heat slithered through her veins.

"No?" she whispered.

"No," he said.

He was right. She wasn't going anywhere. Not tonight. Tomorrow would come soon enough and reason would come with it but for now—for now, there was this. Lucas's mouth on hers. His taste on her tongue. His hand on her breast, his leg between her thighs…

Caroline smiled.

"And how are you going to stop me?" she murmured.

He laughed, low in his throat. Lifted her leg, brought it high over his hip. Teased her with the fullness of his newly aroused flesh rubbing against her sudden wetness until she moaned.

"Lucas."

"Caroline."

Despite this, what he was doing to her, the exquisite torture of it, she was determined to repay his teasing with her own.

"Lucas," she said, "do you really think what you're doing is enough to—is enough to—"

She gasped as he rocked into her.

"I don't know," he said, the roughness of his voice denying the innocence of his words. "Is it?"

"No," she said, and caught her breath as he rocked into her again. Not deeply enough. God, nowhere near deeply enough. "No," she repeated, but the word was a moan.

"Because if it isn't…"

He thrust harder. Deeper. Caroline arched like a bow at the pleasure of it.

"Do you like this?" he said thickly.

"Yes." She framed his face between her hands. "Yes, oh yes!"

"Good. Because I like it, too. I love it. The feel of you all around me. Opening for me. Stretching for me."

"Please," she whispered. "Lucas, please…"

He groaned, drove deep, sank into her until there was no him, no her, no beginning and no end.

And took her with him, to paradise.

The cat woke her.

"Mrrow," it said, in a voice surprisingly delicate for such an arrogant winner of a thousand back-alley fights—but maybe she knew less than she'd assumed about arrogance and tough guys.

Maybe some of them wore those qualities like a shield and only let a handful of people get past it.

"Mrrow," the cat said again, and Caroline sighed.

Oliver—she'd named him for the half-starved, brutalized little boy in Dickens' sad tale—Oliver was right. Middle of the night philosophizing wasn't helpful when there was an immediate problem to solve, and Oliver's problem was probably an empty dinner bowl.

She reached down, felt a ragged ear and caressed it.

"Okay," she whispered, "I'm coming."

Lucas lay sleeping beside her, his arm looped around her shoulders. Slowly, carefully, she eased away from him. He stirred in his sleep, muttered something in Portuguese—she'd finally figured out that what he occasionally spoke was not Spanish but something close to it—and she froze, not wanting to wake him.

That was what she'd done that first night. Awakened suddenly in the dark, stayed absolutely still for fear of waking him, but this was different. She wasn't worried about waking him this time, she simply wanted him to get some sleep. Neither was she shocked at finding herself in his bed...

Okay.

She was. A little. Sleeping with him again—not that they'd done much sleeping—was the last thing she'd ever imagined she would do. Not that she hadn't thought about it. About him. About what he'd made her feel, what being with him had been like.

But she and he came from different worlds. That those worlds had intersected had been a quirk of fate. And then, when fate had brought them together again, at Dani's, Lucas has been so angry, so cold to her, treating her as if she had done something unspeakably wrong. Yes, she'd slipped from his bed that first night but surely that wasn't enough to...

"Mrrow, rorrow, mrrow," the cat said with obvious impatience, and Caroline rose, reached for a silk throw at the foot of the bed, improvised a sarong and padded, barefoot, from the room.

The cat wound around her ankles as she made her way down the stairs. There was just enough light to see where she was going and she remembered the broken glass in the kitchen in time to avoid it.

Oliver avoided it, too, all but tiptoeing his way through

the little minefield of shards. He jumped onto a wicker stool and from there to the white stone counter where he sat, tail curled around his feet, watching Caroline with almond-eyed interest.

First things first, she thought, and she searched for a utility closet, found one, found a dustpan and broom, carefully swept up the glass and dumped it in the trash.

"Now you won't cut yourself," she told the cat, who answered by lifting a paw and licking it.

She checked Oliver's dishes. The water bowl was still full but she emptied it, rinsed it, then refilled it. Just as she'd figured, his food bowl was empty.

"I'm sorry, sweetheart," she said guiltily.

She washed that, too, dried it and filled it with Kitty Krunchies.

*"Meow,"* the cat said politely, and yawned.

Caroline smiled and scooped him into her arms.

"Were you lonely, baby? Is that why you woke me?"

The cat purred and closed his eyes. Caroline kissed the top of his head, wandered out of the kitchen, into the living room and sank down in the corner of a white sofa that surely had cost more than everything she owned.

"It's okay," she said softly. "You have me now. You won't feel lonely ever again."

The cat seemed to grow heavier. His purrs slowed. He was falling asleep, safe in her arms.

Caroline lay her head back.

That was how she'd fallen asleep in Lucas's arms that very first night. They'd made love that second time and he'd held her close and she'd felt an emotion, a state of being, whatever you could call it, that she had never felt before.

She'd felt safe.

Such a strange thing for a grown woman to feel, but there was no other way to describe it. That was why she'd fallen asleep in a strange bed, in a strange man's arms…until she'd awakened and realized that she'd had sex with a stranger…

Caroline's lashes drooped.

Lucas was right. She *had* run away. The reality of what she'd done had been too shameful to bear.

Now, she had done it again, gone to his bed even though he was still little more than a stranger, a stranger who confused her beyond words, talking to her with such tamped-down rage at Dani's, then coming to her rescue, soothing her terror…

Coldness seeped into her bones.

Was she her mother's daughter after all?

It was years since she'd let in those buried memories but they flooded through her now. Mama in their little house just outside town, a new man with her. Mama, bright and happy and excited, certain he was the one.

And, weeks or sometimes months later, the inevitable signs that the affair was running its course. For the man, never for her mother. Mama's Prince Charming would drop by less often. He would call less frequently. He had excuses when Mama invited him to supper.

The only good thing about those times was that, for a little while, Caroline would have her mother to herself; she wouldn't have to pretend she wanted to watch stuff on TV when Mama and the current love of her life went out or, even worse, disappeared into Mama's bedroom.

It happened over and over. Still, when each affair played out to its predictable end, her mother was always devastated. Shocked, to find herself discarded. Not Caroline. She'd been able to read the signs by the time she was eight or nine.

If nothing else, growing up that way, she'd learned something valuable.

You didn't let yourself get involved with a man who thought he owned the world. You didn't treat sex casually. And you certainly didn't give a man all of yourself. Not ever. Bad enough if you gave a man your body, but you never gave away your heart and your soul.

She took a long breath.

Okay. One out of three wasn't so bad.

She was involved with an arrogant man. Some might say she'd treated sex casually. But she absolutely had not, absolutely never would give Lucas anything but her body.

Her heart, her soul, were safe. Completely safe—

"Caroline?"

A light came on. Caroline's eyes flew open. The cat hissed, jumped off her lap and ran.

"*Querida?* What are you doing, sitting alone in the dark?"

Lucas stood in the center of the living room, naked except for a pair of sweatpants, his dark hair tousled, his face shadowed by that sexy end-of-day stubble she'd felt beneath her fingers.

Her heart thudded.

He was so beautiful. So much more than beautiful. Just seeing him scattered her doubts, made her think only of what it was like to be in his arms.

"I thought you'd left me again," he said, as he came toward her. He bent and kissed her, his lips taking hers with possessive hunger.

"This time," he said in a rough voice, "this time, I would have come after you."

She looked up at him. She wanted to say something clever and sophisticated. Instead, what she was thinking tumbled from her mouth.

"Then—then, why didn't you last time?"

He nodded, as if she'd asked him to explain some complex mathematical formula.

"Lucas? Why didn't you look for me?"

He nodded again and ran his hand through his hair.

It was an excellent question. Why hadn't he sought her out the morning she'd left his bed?

Ego, at first. Women did not walk out on him. Going after her would have damaged his pride. Stupid, but there it was.

Then, after Jack Gordon told him more about Dani Sinclair, after he'd put two and two together and figured out what Caroline was…

*If* that was what she was. Only if…but still, how could he tell her that?

How could he say, *I couldn't go after you because it kills me to think of you with other men. Because I am too proud to have ever imagined myself in such a situation. Because, even now, a part of me wonders if you are acting, if sex is a performance for you, if what you said was true, that the night you were with me was truly the first time you had sold yourself…*

It must have been, he thought fiercely. A woman whose profession was sex would not cry out with shock when he parted her thighs, sought the delicate bud between them, teased it with his tongue. She would not blush under the intensity of his gaze when he drew back and said he wanted to watch her face as he made love to her…

"Lucas? You didn't look for me and yet, today, you insisted I come home with you." Caroline swallowed dryly; he saw the muscles in her throat constrict. "It doesn't make sense."

No. It did not. None of it did. He only knew that she belonged with him. That he wanted her with him. That he had told himself he'd gone to her apartment for closure when the truth was, he'd gone there for her.

"Perhaps we're looking for logic where there is none," he said softly. He took her hands in his, drew her to her feet. "All that matters is that I did come after you this time. And now, we are together." He smiled as he drew her to him, hoping to ease the darkness from her eyes. "You, and me, and a cat that is sitting in a corner, plotting how to get rid of me."

Caroline laughed, as he'd hoped she would.

"He'll come around, you'll see. It won't take more than a couple of days. By the time I leave here—"

"You're not leaving."

"Not tonight, no. I meant, when I find an apartment…"

Lucas sat down on the sofa and drew her into his lap. "Let's not talk about that now," he said softly.

No. She didn't want to talk about it, either.

"All right." She smiled. "Let's talk about you."

He looked startled. "Me?"

"I don't know anything about you." She smiled again. "Well, I know that you can read a menu written in hyperbole."

Lucas laughed. "Harder to read than Russian, huh?"

"Definitely." She lowered her lashes, batted them at him. *"Mais, monsieur, je peux lire un menu en français très bien."*

"Very nice." He smiled, brushed his lips over hers. "I'm impressed."

Caroline sighed. "Me, too. Not so much that I can speak and read French and Russian, that I ever had the chance to learn them at all."

"Meaning?"

She gave a little shrug.

"Well, I grew up in a small town."

Yes, he almost said, I know. He stopped himself just in time.

"It was the kind of place where your life was, I don't know, I guess it was sort of planned for you." She lay her head against his shoulder. "The banker's son was going to go to college, come home and be a banker. The baker's daughter was going to go to a two-year college, study nutrition and—"

"And, come home and be a baker."

Caroline gave a soft laugh.

"Exactly." She touched a finger to his jaw, rubbed it over the dark stubble. "There was a plant in town that made garden tractors. My mother worked there, on the assembly line." Her smile tilted. "In high school, I signed up to take French. And my guidance counselor called me down to his office and said I'd be better off taking cosmetology or shop because what good would French do me after I graduated and my mother got me a job working beside her?"

Lucas nodded calmly while he envisioned going to Caroline's hometown, finding the counselor and beating the crap out of him.

"But you had no intention of working in that factory," he said.

"Not for a second. I wanted something—something—"

"Better?"

"Something more."

He nodded. "So you told the counselor what he could do with his advice and signed up for French."

She grinned. It was the kind of grin that gave him a glimpse of the kid she must have been: beautiful, defiant, determined.

"I was tactful but basically, I guess that's just what I told him." Her face grew serious. "One thing I learned, growing up, was that you have to take care of yourself in this world."

They had that in common, he thought, and wished, for her sake, that they didn't.

"And," he said, keeping things light, "you turned out to be a genius at French."

"I turned out to be a good student. I won a scholarship, came to New York—"

"But New York wasn't quite what you'd expected."

"It was more than I'd expected. Big. Wonderful. Exciting."

"And expensive."

Was that a subtle change in his tone?

"Well, yes. Very. Back home—"

"Back home, that scholarship money had seemed enormous but when you got to the city, you had to supplement it."

"Of course."

"And so you did," he said, and now, there was no mistaking the change in his voice.

Did he know she waited tables? Did he think less of her for that?

"People do what they have to do," she said quietly. "A man like you might not understand that, but—"

Lucas cursed, cupped one big hand behind her head and brought her mouth to his. At first, all she did was accept his kiss. Then her lips softened and parted; he tasted the sweetness of her and after he ended the kiss, he gathered her against his heart.

He was no one to sit in judgment. His childhood had been one of doing what he had to do to survive. Petty thefts. Food snatched from market stands. Wallets lifted from the pockets of fat tourists. Who knew what more he might have done, as the years went by?

She was right.

People did what they had to do to survive.

Besides, all that was in the past. He'd never let her return to her former life, not even after—after their time together had run its course. He couldn't know when that day would come but it always did. And when that happened, he'd see that she was safe. An apartment. A job. He knew people everywhere who could surely offer solid employment to such a bright young woman.

He sensed it wouldn't be easy to convince her to accept his help but he'd find a way to do it. She would see that his wanting to help her was a good thing.

For now, they would be together. That was all that was important.

"See?" he said lightly. "I've learned something about you, and you've learned something about me."

"No," she said, her eyes on his, "I haven't."

"Sure you have. You've learned that I'm a bear before I have my morning coffee."

His tone was carefree but Caroline knew it was a cover-up. He didn't want to talk about himself. She wanted to know more, to know him, but for now, just being with him was enough. So she smiled and gave him a quick kiss.

"In that case, let's go make coffee."

She rose to her feet. The silk sarong she'd improvised slipped, exposing her breasts. She grabbed for it but Lucas caught her wrists, drew them to her sides.

In a heartbeat, the mood of the moment changed.

"Coffee. *Sim.* But first, just a taste of you."

He drew a rose-pink nipple into his mouth. Carolyn caught her breath.

"Do you like that?" he whispered.

"I love it. The feel of your mouth—"

With deft fingers, he undid the knot in the silk throw. It slipped to her feet, leaving her naked.

"Caroline. *Meu amor.* You are so beautiful. So beautiful…"

He stood and gathered her against him. She felt the swift hardening of his flesh.

That she could do this to him thrilled her.

That he would soon be inside her, moving inside her, thrilled her even more.

She put her hand between them. He made a rough sound in the back of his throat. Her fingers danced the length of his penis. She could feel his flesh pulse beneath the soft cotton sweats.

"Caroline." His voice carried a warming. "If you keep doing that—"

She put her hands at his hips, slowly eased the sweatpants down. She watched his face, loved the darkening of his eyes, the narrowing of his mouth.

"Caroline," he said hoarsely. "Do you have any idea what—"

Her hand closed around him. He groaned. He was silk and steel, incredible softness laid over all that raw masculine hardness.

She had never touched a man this way before, had never even imagined wanting to. But she wanted to know everything about her lover. If he wouldn't talk about himself, she would find other ways to explore him.

Like this.

Caroline dropped to her knees. Held him in her hands. Licked his length. Touched the tip of her tongue to his swollen sex.

Lucas shuddered. His hands threaded into her hair. He rocked back on his heels, groaning, and then he reached for her, drew her to her feet, tumbled her back on the white silk sofa and plunged into her.

She came instantly.

So did he.

He thought, as he held her, that what she had just done for him, to him, was wonderful.

And then he thought, *How many times has she done it before?*

His gut twisted.

He rose to his feet, plucked the silk throw from the carpet and covered her with it.

"Lucas?" she said, and sat up.

He smiled, and it was one of the most difficult things he'd ever done.

"Let me bring you a robe," he said brightly. "Then we'll have breakfast."

He thought he sounded cheerful but when he came back with a robe, he saw that she had wrapped the discarded silk throw around herself. That, and the look on her face, told him he hadn't pulled it off.

"Caroline. Sweetheart—"

"What is it? What's the matter? Did I—did I do something—what I just did, was it—"

Her eyes glittered with unshed tears, her mouth trembled. How could he have thought, even for a second, that she had done this with other men? Cursing himself, he reached for her, took her in his arms and kissed her.

"What did I tell you, *querida*? A bear before coffee, *sim*?" He kissed her again, kept kissing her until her body softened against his and the doubt had left her eyes. "I'm going to make you the best breakfast you ever had. It's the national dish of Brazil. Bacon and waffles, with maple syrup."

The foolish joke worked. A smile curved her lips.

"Waffles are not the national dish of anywhere!"

"But they should be, because I make the best waffles in the world."

Her eyebrows rose. "Really."

"Really. And the best coffee."

"If you're going to make the coffee and the waffles, what's left for me to do?"

"You'll have a very important job."

"Which is?"

"You're going to make my kitchen look beautiful."

She laughed. "That certainly does sound important."

"Very important," he said solemnly. "And I'm sure you're going to be very good at it."

Just as he was going to be very good at forgetting what he

knew about her past. Or wondering about it. Hadn't he learned that as a boy?

Who you were at the beginning of your life meant nothing.

It was who you ultimately became that mattered.

# CHAPTER NINE

THEY showered. Put on robes.

And had breakfast.

Breakfast took a long time.

It had to, when every mouthful was interspersed with soft, teasing kisses that tasted of maple syrup.

Lucas made the waffles and coffee. Caroline found a real job to do, after all. She made the bacon. She said his waffles were heavenly. He said he had never tasted bacon so delicious.

"Thank you, sir," she said demurely. "That compliment almost justifies the time I've spent in greasy-spoon kitchens." She smiled. "Notice, I said 'almost.'"

"Greasy-spoon kitchens?" Lucas drank some coffee. "What kind are those?"

Caroline laughed.

"Not the kind you'd know, I'm sure."

"You mean," he said with wide-eyed innocence, "not one that would be found in that restaurant the night we met?"

It was the first reference either of them had made to the start of that evening, and he'd made it with as much grace as if they'd been on a real date, not a pretend one.

"No," she said softly, "not like that place at all."

"Ah." He grinned. "I didn't think so."

Caroline ate a bit of waffle. A drop of syrup glittered in

the very center of her bottom lip. Lucas leaned toward her and licked it away, loving the way she caught her breath as he did, loving it enough to cover her mouth with his and turn the moment of contact into a real kiss.

"Maple syrup," he said softly. "I wanted to make sure it didn't drip."

She smiled. "That's very kind of you," she said, just as softly. "Let me return the compliment."

She cupped her hand around the back of his head, brought his face to hers again and kissed him, her mouth soft beneath his. He cupped her face, his fingers threading into her hair, and took the kiss deep. After endless seconds, she drew back.

*Deus*, he loved it when she looked like this, cheeks rosy, mouth delicately swollen, eyes filled with him.

"The waffles will get cold," she whispered.

Lucas was on the verge of saying he didn't give a damn if they turned to ice. From the look on her face, he doubted if she did, either…

"Good morning, Mr. Vieira."

Startled, Caroline jumped. Lucas bit back a curse. He'd forgotten his housekeeper would be coming in this morning.

He turned toward her and thought, with amusement, that Mrs. Kennelly would make an excellent poker player. Nothing showed in her placid face even though she'd never before found him at breakfast with a woman.

And then he thought, *Deus*, he was at breakfast. With a woman. Here, in his own kitchen.

It was a first.

Women sometimes spent the night, sure. And, early in the morning, they left. Oh, on Sundays he might take a woman who'd spent the night to brunch but this, sitting in his own kitchen, sharing a meal they'd prepared together…

Caroline was getting ready to bolt. He could feel it. Calmly, as if nothing unusual had happened, he reached for her hand.

"Good morning, Mrs. Kennelly. Caroline, this is Mrs. Kennelly. My housekeeper."

He looked at Caroline. She was pink with embarrassment. That made him want to kiss her, which made no sense. Besides, that would only add to her embarrassment so he clasped her hand more tightly and wove his fingers through hers.

Mrs. Kennelly smiled politely. "How do you do, miss?"

He heard Caroline's deep intake of breath, saw the proud lift of her chin.

"It's nice to meet you, Mrs. Kennelly."

"Miss Hamilton is going to be staying with us for a while."

Caroline shot him a look.

"No," she said in a low voice, "really, I'm—"

Lucas rose to his feet, his hand still holding hers, and drew her up beside him.

"We'll get out of your way, Mrs. Kennelly," he said pleasantly. "Isn't that right, sweetheart?"

Only if getting out of the way meant the floor would open and swallow her, Caroline thought frantically.

How did a woman deal with a scene like this?

Lucas was composed. So was his housekeeper. She was the only one who wanted to die, and wasn't that ridiculous? She had spent the night in bed with him, doing things. Wonderful, exciting things.

And now what horrified her was his housekeeper finding her in his robe, in his kitchen?

But then, why would Lucas or Mrs. Kennelly be horrified? This scene had to be fairly commonplace for a man like him.

Trouble was, it was anything but for a woman like her. She

had never even spent the night with a man before, much less faced his housekeeper the next morning.

"Caroline?"

She blinked. Lucas smiled at her.

"Let's let Mrs. Kennelly get started, *sim*?"

That "sim" was meaningful. Lucas rarely used Portuguese. He spoke it when he was angry. When he made love to her. And that "sim," a word she figured meant "yes," crept in every once in a while but only when he was determined to make a point and right now, the point was that he wanted her to behave like a grown-up. So she did. She let him draw her from the stool while she forced what she hoped was a smile.

"Of course. Just let me clean up before—"

"Nonsense, miss," the housekeeper said briskly. "You go on. I'll take care of this."

Well, of course. If she didn't know how to behave by being found all but naked in a man's kitchen, she surely didn't know how to behave around a housekeeper.

The best thing was to keep smiling, to keep holding Lucas's hand or, rather, to let him hold hers, to follow him through the sunny penthouse, to the steps, up the steps, down the hall, to his bedroom...

And to remember, all too quickly, what she was doing here, that she didn't belong here, that she'd made one mistake after another where Lucas Vieira was concerned.

Actually, his housekeeper's appearance was a very good thing.

Lucas shut the door. Let go of her hand. Folded his arms and looked at her. What was he going to say? She couldn't imagine. And it wouldn't matter. She was going to speak first.

"Lucas."

He raised an eyebrow. She hated when he did that. Actually, she loved it. It made him look dangerous and sexy, although he looked dangerous and sexy enough without doing anything at all.

"Lucas," she said again, "I—"

"My housekeeper is a better poker player than you are."

"Excuse me?"

"She saw you and showed no reaction. You saw her and looked as if you wished the floor would open and swallow you."

Did he read minds? Caroline mimicked his action, folded her arms and looked straight at him.

"I was—surprised."

Lucas's mouth twitched. "I'd never have known."

Her eyes narrowed. "You might find this amusing. I don't."

"I find it—interesting."

That tiny muscle flickered in his jaw. Whenever it did, she had an almost overwhelming desire to run up to him and press her lips to his skin.

Which was the last thing she should be thinking right now.

"To hell with interesting," she said briskly. "I had it right the first time. You find this amusing."

"Wrong, *querida*. A man who has never shared breakfast with a woman in his very own kitchen and who suddenly realizes it when his housekeeper discovers him doing so, does not find the situation amusing."

Caroline blinked. "Never?"

"Never what?"

"Never both things. I mean— You've never had breakfast here with a—with a woman before?"

Lucas shrugged. "No."

"But—"

"I am not a man who does such things."

"But—"

"You already said that."

"I know I did. I just don't understand why you—"

"No." His voice was suddenly low and rough. "I don't understand it, either." His arms fell to his sides. Slowly, he came toward her, his eyes hot. "I don't understand any of it."

Caroline's heart began to race.

"What don't you understand?" she whispered.

Lucas gathered her into his arms. She sighed as he drew her against him and when she did, he thought it was the most perfect sound he'd ever heard a woman make.

"You," he said. "Me. This."

He groaned, brought her to her toes and claimed her mouth with his.

What he'd offered was not an answer and yet it was the only answer he had, the only one he could give, the only one that made sense.

"Lucas," she said unsteadily, "Lucas…"

Slowly, he opened the sash of her robe. His robe, he thought. His. The robe slid from her shoulders and he looked at her, the lovely face and body that were without artifice.

He told her she was beautiful. That she was perfect. He told it to her in Portuguese, told her, too, how much he wanted her.

He could see the pulse beating in the hollow of her throat.

"What about—what about Mrs. Kennelly?"

Despite everything—his desire, his passion, the almost painful hardening of his flesh—he laughed.

"We won't tell her," he said softly, and Caroline stared at him and then, to his delight, she giggled.

"Such a good idea," she said.

And then her smile changed, her hazel eyes darkened and

she reached for him, lay her hand over him where his aroused flesh swelled and throbbed.

"Make love to me," she whispered, and he lifted her in his arms. Carried her to his bed. Lay her down so that her hair was a halo of gold against the pillows and then he pulled off his sweatpants, kicked them aside, came down over her and made love to her with such care, such tenderness that when it was over, Caroline wept.

And Lucas—

He held her close, felt her heart beating against his, her breath on his throat, and he stroked her and kissed her and wondered what in hell was happening to him.

He had to go to work.

People, appointments, emails and phone calls and paper-work were waiting for him.

He told it to himself. He told it to Caroline.

"Of course," she said.

"Of course," he said solemnly. Then he reached past her for the bedside phone, called his P.A., told her he would not be in and that she could reach him on his cell if something important came up.

"Something vital," he said, just to clarify things. He paused. "On second thought, don't call me at all."

He hung up, laughing at what he knew had to be the look on his P.A.'s face.

"What's funny?" Caroline asked, and Lucas kissed her, kissed her again and blew bubbles against her belly button and she laughed and he looked up and suddenly knew that he had never been happier in his entire life.

The thought stilled his laughter.

"What?" Caroline said, but there was nothing he could say that would not be dangerous so he scooped her up. "Where are you taking me? Lucas. Lucas! Where…?"

She shrieked as he stepped into the shower stall with her in his arms, turned on all the sprays until they were cocooned in a warm, delicious waterfall, and her pretended protests faded as he kissed her, set her on her feet, kissed her breasts and slid his hand between her thighs.

"Lucas," she whispered.

"What, sweetheart?" he said, against her mouth, but she had no answer, none she could afford to give him, because she was happy, so happy, and she knew happiness like this couldn't last…

"Put your arms around me," he said. And he stepped back against the wall, lifted her and she wrapped her legs around him and then there were no questions, no answers, none were needed because they were lost in each other's arms.

Caroline fed Oliver. Changed the water in his bowl. Opened a Daintee Deelites. Scooped out his litter pan.

The cat purred and wove around her ankles.

"I'll see you soon, baby," she cooed as she picked him up and kissed his head while the cat and Lucas eyed each other in silent communication.

His driver took them to Caroline's apartment.

Lucas wasn't happy about it.

"I don't like the thought of you being here," he said, "even for a little while."

Caroline didn't answer. What would she say? Yesterday, she'd agreed she couldn't go on living in this place. Today, she was calmer. She knew she had little choice. It had taken forever to find her apartment; affordable rents were tough enough in Manhattan but when "affordable" referred to the stipend she received as a teaching assistant and her earnings as a waitress—and she'd have to find another job, and quickly— when that was the meaning of "affordable," the miserable rooms she already had were better than most others.

She'd thought about the problem on the way and she'd come up with a simple plan. She'd accept Lucas's hospitality for a couple of days. Three, at the most. And she'd look for an apartment. If she didn't find one—and she was willing to bet that she wouldn't—she'd move back here.

She already knew better than to tell that to Lucas.

Instead, she offered a noncommittal "Mmm," and obeyed his command to give him her keys and stand in back of him when he opened the door to her apartment.

"Command" was the only way to describe that macho arrogance.

That oh-so-sexy macho arrogance.

The door opened. Lucas stepped into the living room, then motioned her forward.

The room was as she'd left it. No, not quite. The super had installed a new window as well as a locking window gate. That, at least, made her feel better.

It didn't do a thing for Lucas, who shut the door, strode to the window, clamped his hand around the top of the iron gate and shook it.

"Too little, too late," he growled.

"It seems sturdy enough."

"Maybe. But the locks on the door wouldn't stop an amateur."

Okay. This wasn't going to be a fruitful discussion. Besides, there was no point to it. Lucas lived on a different planet. He could never understand her life, and she didn't expect him to.

Instead of answering, she went into the tiny bedroom and opened the closet, began pulling things from hangers, the few garments she'd need for the next few apartment-hunting days.

Lucas cleared his throat.

"You know," he said, "you could leave all that here and, ah, and start fresh."

Caroline looked at him. "No," she said, "I could not."

He opened his mouth, then shut it. A good thing, too. Did he actually think she could afford to toss these things out and buy new ones? He was not just from another planet, he was from another galaxy.

She turned back to the closet, added two pairs of shoes and a purse to the small stack of items she'd put on the bed.

What else?

Some of her textbooks. Her laptop computer. A stack of printed notes. She put them all into a backpack, stuffed the clothes, shoes and purse into a canvas messenger bag, took a last look around and swung toward Lucas.

"There," she said, "that'll…" The look on his face silenced her. He was looking around him as if he'd never seen a place so small, so pitiful before. And, yes, it was both those things, but it was honest, it was hers, she had paid for it all, and she wasn't in anyone's debt.

"Is there a problem?"

She'd meant to sound coolly amused. Instead, she sounded just plain cool.

He looked at her.

"You should not have to live like this," he said gruffly.

Caroline folded her arms. "Not everyone can live in the sky."

"In the…? My condo, you mean."

"Yes. I know it must come as a terrible surprise but in the real world—"

"Don't take that tone with me!"

"I'll take any tone I like! As I said, in the real world—"

"I know all about the real world, damnit!" He was on her in two strides, clasping her elbows, lifting her to her toes, his head lowered so their eyes were on the same level. "Do you think I was born, as you put it, in the sky?"

"Let go of me."

"Answer the question. Do you think I was always rich?" His mouth twisted. "Do you know what a *favela* is?"

She stared at him. "I've heard the word. It's a—a Brazilian slum."

Lucas gave a bitter laugh. "A slum is much higher on the socio-economic ladder, *querida*."

He was upset. Very upset. Caroline's anger faded.

"Lucas. I didn't mean to pry."

"I was born in a shack with a tin roof. A couple of years later, things got really bad and we traded that for what was, basically, a cardboard box in an alley."

Her eyebrows rose. Was it in shock at what he was saying, or because his tone was curt? And why was he telling her this? No one knew his story. It wasn't that he was ashamed of it.

Not exactly.

It was just that it wasn't pretty. The poverty. The abandonment by his mother. The foster homes.

The thefts. The pockets he'd picked. Ugly and, yes, he was ashamed. Besides, his personal life was his; he saw no reason to share it with anyone else.

And yet—and yet—

For the first time ever, he felt the temptation to tell someone who he was. Who he really was. People knew him as he presented himself, a man rich almost beyond comprehension, in full command of his own life and, though it was a daunting realization, in command of the lives of others, as well.

But sometimes, in the deepest part of the night, he wondered how people would view him if they knew that he had become that man after a beginning a caseworker in the first shelter that had taken him in had called "humble" when the truth was, his beginnings had not been humble but squalid.

How would Caroline see him if she knew all the details? What would she think of him? Was the Lucas Vieira she cared for rich and powerful, or was he simply a man?

And what in hell was he doing, thinking any of this? What was he doing, thinking Caroline cared for him? She liked him, yes. She was grateful to him for what he had done yesterday. And she liked having sex with him, or she seemed to, unless that was all an act, unless it was yet another part of the game they'd played from that first night…

"Lucas?"

He blinked and looked at her.

"You don't know me, Caroline. You don't know a damned thing about me."

"No." Her voice was low. She reached up, lay her palm against his jaw. "I don't. The truth is, we don't know anything about each other."

For an instant, the tension in him had eased. Now, she felt it return.

"You're right," he said. "For instance, I don't understand why you live in a place like this."

Caroline snatched back her hand. "Because it's what I can afford on a TA's salary. On a waitress's tips. For a man who claims he grew up in poverty, you don't understand much."

Lucas's hands tightened on her.

"Is that all you do? Teach? Wait on tables?"

"What's that supposed to mean?"

"I gave you a thousand dollars."

A flush rose in her face. "You mean, you paid me a thousand dollars for a night's work."

His jaw tightened. "Indeed."

"And, what? That gives you the right to ask what I did with it?"

It didn't. He knew that. He knew he was on the verge of saying something he would regret but he had questions, endless questions. Yesterday, he'd been so fixed on the danger of where Caroline lived, on what had almost happened to her, that he hadn't thought of anything else.

Now, he saw the real poverty of her furnishings. The drabness of her clothes.

What did she do with the money she earned selling herself? *If* she sold herself. He had to keep that "if" in mind.

"Lucas."

Dani Sinclair's fee for a night was many times what he had paid Caroline. Caroline's should have been twenty times more than that.

She was everything a man could want, in bed and out. Warm and sweet and funny. Giving and loving and exciting.

The way she laughed at his jokes. Complimented his cooking. Sighed in his arms and gave herself so completely when they made love. Even her devotion to The Cat from Hell, to that pathetic fern...

How could she be a woman who sold herself? How could she give herself to anyone but him? And that was what this was all about. That he wanted her to give herself only to him...

"Lucas. You're hurting me!"

He looked at his hands, gripping her shoulders so hard that he could feel each finger digging into her flesh.

*Deus*, he was losing his mind!

Carefully, he let go of her. She started to step back and he shook his head, lightly clasped her wrists and drew her to him.

"Caroline." His voice was low. "*Querida*. Forgive me."

He could see the shine of tears in her eyes.

"I don't understand," she said in a shaky voice. "What is it you want from me?"

He held her gaze for a long minute as he searched for an answer, not only for her but for himself. Then, gently, he ran his thumb over the curve of her lower lip, bent his head and pressed a kiss to it.

"I want you," he said softly. "Only you."

He kissed her. She didn't respond. He kissed her again, whispered her name. And, finally, Caroline kissed him back.

That was all she wanted. Lucas's kisses. His arms, holding her to him. Those simple things, and the dizzying realization that something as exhilarating as it was terrifying was happening to her.

That it was happening to—there was no other word for it—to her heart.

# CHAPTER TEN

WEDNESDAY morning, Lucas phoned his office again and told his P.A. that he wouldn't be coming in.

"Cancel all my appointments, please."

Was there a split second of hesitancy before she said, "Yes, Mr. Vieira."

No. Why would there be? They had a pleasant relationship but he was her employer; she never questioned anything he said or did.

But he had never stayed out of the office two days in a row unless it was because he was away on business.

Never, he thought. His behavior was...unusual.

But necessary.

He had things to do. Caroline had mentioned that the semester was over; she had an office at the university.

"Half a closet, actually," she'd said with a quick smile.

She had to pack her books and files, move them out. She didn't ask but, of course, he had to help her. He also had to convince her that she couldn't transport them to her apartment. That was out of the question. He didn't want her in that place for a second, or taking endless subway trips, her arms loaded with boxes, or climbing the dark stairs to those miserable rooms in that building she had called home.

And he had to find a way to keep her from looking for a place to live.

She talked about that, too. Whenever she did, he changed the subject.

He knew she'd have to go out on her own sooner or later. He wanted that, too. At least, he *didn't* want the alternative, a woman living with him, sharing his meals, his quiet mornings, his evenings.

His life.

But it was surprisingly pleasant. For now. Pleasant, surely only because it was a new experience, having her clothes in the guest room closet, her makeup, her hairbrush, all her things in the guest bath. Silly, really, because she spent the nights with him.

In his bed. In his arms.

But it couldn't be a long-term solution.

Of course, it couldn't.

Not a problem.

He had the Realtor looking for that apartment. Someplace bright and safe. Someplace nearby. And he'd called Saks Fifth Avenue, asked to speak to a personal shopper and been put through to someone who sounded efficient.

"I'll need clothes for a, uh, a young woman," he'd said, speaking briskly because he'd suddenly felt foolish.

"Certainly, sir," the personal shopper replied, as if this kind of thing happened all the time. Maybe it did, but the experience was brand-new for Lucas.

"The lady's size?"

"She's a six," he'd said, because he'd anticipated the question and he'd taken a quick look at the labels in some of Caroline's things.

"Her height?"

Height. A difficult question. *Tall enough to come up to my heart when she's barefoot*, he'd almost said, and caught himself just in time.

"Average," was his answer, even though there was nothing

"average" about his Caroline, but the answer seemed to satisfy
the personal shopper.

"And her style, sir."

"Her style?"

"Yes. Is she into current fashion? Does she like a glamorous
look? Has she any favorite designers?"

His Caroline's style was strictly her own. Easy. Simple.
As for designers, from what he could tell, she chose them by
price tag.

"She, ah, she prefers a casual look."

And then he thought of the spectacular outfit she'd worn
the night they met—and he thought, too, that of everything
he'd seen in the guest room closet when he'd checked her
clothing for size, he had not seen anything remotely close to
that short, leg-baring dress or the sky-high stilettos.

"But she looks amazing in other things, too," he'd added.
"Silk dresses. Skinny heels. Soft, feminine stuff…"

*Deus*, he'd thought, almost groaning with embarrassment.

The shopper had come to his rescue.

"You've given me an excellent portrait to work with," she'd
said pleasantly.

Lucas certainly hoped so. Going through this again would
be hell.

He told her to charge everything to his black Amex card
and to wait for delivery until he called with an address. So
that was taken care of. Clothes and, soon, an apartment. He
thought about how pleased Caroline would be with those
surprises.

She would be pleased, wouldn't she?

Of course, she would.

But he couldn't surprise her when it came to packing up
her office stuff. Only she'd know what she wanted to take and
what she wanted to leave.

He'd considered having his driver take her uptown to the university campus.

Then he thought how much simpler it would be if he did it instead.

He kept a red Ferrari 599 in a garage a few blocks away. He loved the car's elegant lines and incredible power but he hadn't had much chance to drive it. Business took up more and more of his life.

This would be a good opportunity to put some mileage on the Ferrari.

All in all, it made sense to take the day off.

They made breakfast together again. He'd decided to give Mrs. Kennelly the week off, with a month's pay. She deserved it and, yes, if it meant he had his penthouse all to himself, he and Caroline, that he could make love to her wherever, whenever they both wanted, well, that was simply a coincidental benefit.

It was the kind of morning that made June in New York close to perfect, and they took their coffee out to the terrace. Lucas told Caroline the plans he'd made for the day.

She smiled. "It's a very sweet offer."

And while he was still wondering when anyone had ever called anything he'd done "sweet," she added that she didn't want him to turn his schedule inside out for her.

"I'm not," he said, with calm self-assurance. "And you'll be doing me a favor."

Caroline raised her eyebrows. "I will?"

"The car really needs to be driven. My mechanic says so."

She looked dubious. No wonder. It was a lie but how could he tell her that turning his schedule inside out seemed far less important than being separated for her, even for a day?

Where had that thought come from? Although, *sim*, it made a kind of sense. Their relationship was so new…

No. It wasn't a relationship. He didn't have "relationships." It was simply—it was just—it was something but he couldn't manage to call it an "affair," not with the cool sophistication the term implied.

Caroline lay her hand over his.

"Then, thank you," she said softly, and he heard himself say, with a roughness that caught him off-guard, that if she really wanted to thank him she could offer him a kiss, just a little kiss, and she laughed and leaned over the table and pressed her lips gently to his and then it was a good thing, a very good thing that Mrs. Kennelly wasn't there because Lucas got to his feet, swept Caroline into his arms, carried her to a chaise longue and took her under the soft June sky with a ferocity that turned to tenderness with such breathtaking speed that when she reached orgasm, tears glittered in her eyes. And he—

He felt something happen, deep in his heart.

When she began to rise, he shook his head.

"Don't go," he said softly, and he held her cradled against him, the warmth of her skin kissing his, the delicate scent of her in his nostrils, and he thought how amazing it was that he was a grown man, that sex—great sex—had been part of his life for years…

But it had never been like this.

They showered and dressed, both of them in jeans and T-shirts, Lucas with a cashmere sweater over his shirt, Caroline with a hoodie over hers.

She looked beautiful and he told her so, and though he knew that nothing could ever improve her beauty because it was already perfect, the silks and cashmeres the personal shopper would provide would be the right touch for her lovely face and feminine curves.

He phoned his garage. The car was ready when they arrived, long and sleek and red, as high-spirited as a race horse.

"Oh," Caroline said softly, "oh, my! It's beautiful!"

He grinned. "And fast."

"I'll bet. It looks like it's moving, even standing still. What did you say it was?"

"A Ferrari. A Ferrari 599."

She wrinkled her brow. "What's that mean, exactly?"

So he explained. Exactly. The engine specs. The paint. The customization. He explained his car in detail even though he knew, from past experience, that what women wanted to know was if whatever he drove was as expensive as it looked.

But Caroline listened. Asked questions. And once they were moving through the Manhattan streets—slowly, because of traffic, though he could almost feel the car trying to break free—once they were moving, he found himself describing the first car he'd ever owned.

"It was a clunker."

She laughed. "A clunker, huh?"

"Absolutely. It was older than I was."

She laughed again. "It's hard to imagine you driving something like that."

"Hey, I loved that car. It took me wherever I wanted to go—as long as I pulled over every fifty miles and added a can of oil."

They both laughed, and Lucas thought how amazing it was that he'd remembered that old car, much less told her the story. He never shared anything from his past with anyone, it just wasn't what he did, and yet, in a few short days, he'd revealed more about himself to Caroline than he ever had before.

What would she think if she knew his entire story? That his mother had abandoned him. That he'd survived by being a thief and a con artist. That he'd run from the cops. That he'd grown up in foster homes where sometimes, same as in the streets, nothing mattered but survival.

When he'd first come to the States, tough and street-hardened, unwilling to let anybody or anything get past the barriers he'd built, a well-meaning counselor who treated kids like him told him that he had to accept his past before he could address his future, that pretending bad things had never happened to him was like living a lie…

"But you lied to me, Lucas."

Shocked, he looked at Caroline. "No," he said quickly, "never."

Then the look on her face registered. She was teasing him. The breath eased from his lungs.

"You said you'd help me move my stuff."

"And I will."

"Not in this beautiful beast. It's far too handsome to be filled with boxes. Besides, even if we wanted to, there's no room."

Lucas tried for a look of wounded innocence.

"It's more spacious than you think, *querida*."

She craned her neck and looked at the nonexistent space behind them.

"Uh-huh."

"It is. You'll see."

It wasn't, but what else could he say? Could he tell her he wanted to share his pleasure in the car with her? That being with her, sharing with her, was what mattered?

"And how are you going to park? Where? You can't leave this car on the street."

She was being practical, which was more than he could say of himself. Of course he couldn't leave the Ferrari on the street.

Well, actually, he could.

He loved the car. Its lines, its grace, its speed. He had

worked long and hard for it. But loving an inanimate object wasn't the same as loving a woman.

Not that he knew what loving a woman was like, he thought quickly. Not that he ever wanted to know. Love was a fake word, invented by frauds. It was a concept at best, nothing more. He understood that. He had always understood that, at least since his mother had taught it to him that day she'd left him on a street in Copacabana...

"Lucas." Caroline laughed and poked him with her elbow. "You just drove right past campus."

He had, indeed. Where was his head? Not on his work, or the appointments he'd canceled, or anything useful.

He frowned.

What in hell was he doing? Behaving like a kid with a crush when he was a man with a multibillion dollar empire to run.

His hands flexed on the steering wheel.

It was still early. Plenty of time to head back downtown, garage the car, arrange for James to shuttle Caroline and her cartons while he changed into a suit, went to his office, got some work done.

"You're right," he said. "The car's too small, and where would I park it in this area?"

She nodded. "That's what I thought," she said, in a very soft voice. "This was a lovely idea, but—"

"But completely impractical." Ahead, the light changed, went from red to green. He'd make a left at the intersection, head back toward Fifth Avenue.

He reached the intersection—and said something under his breath as he wrenched the wheel right, not left, and headed for the Long Island Expressway.

He reached for Caroline's hand. Her fingers curled tightly with his.

"Forget about packing your things," he said gruffly. "It's too nice a day for that."

"Then, where are we going?"

"I have a house…"

He fell silent. He'd bought his house in the Hamptons a couple of years ago. The towns on the southeastern end of Long Island were charming, the beaches magnificent, and they were within a couple of hours of the city.

The rich and famous kept summer homes there.

That had influenced him, not because he wanted any part of that world but because he'd heard that people in the Hamptons understood the value of privacy.

If you wanted to be left alone, you were. Lucas wanted exactly that. For him, the place would be a retreat. Sand. Sea. The vastness of the blue sky.

It had turned out to be all that.

It was also lonely.

The house was big. The ocean was endless. Without his work to keep him busy, he'd felt unsettled. Maybe that was the reason he'd spent a couple of weekends there with women he'd been seeing at the time.

Two women. Two weekends. And that had been enough.

He'd been foolish to expect that sand and sea and sky were things women would see as entertainment.

Was he about to make the same mistake again? It had been annoying those other times but if Caroline wasn't happy in his house by the sea…

"A house?" she said. "Where?"

He looked at her. The windows were all open; sunlight glinted on her face and her hair. The moment was so perfect that he wanted to pull to the curb and take her in his arms but in New York traffic, he'd have needed an armored truck, not a Ferrari, to make that happen.

"I have a place on the beach. In the Hamptons. The caretaker keeps it open for me year-round."

"What's it like? Your house?"

He shrugged. The truth was, he loved the house the way he loved the Ferrari.

"It's okay," he said. "Just, you know, a beach house. Lots of glass. A deck. A pool. And the sea."

Caroline sighed. "That's it?"

His heart fell just a little.

"That's it." He cleared his throat. "You know, it's probably not a great idea. Going out there, I mean. It's still early in the season and the weather's kind of cool. Plus, it's midweek. Lots of the clubs will be closed, and—"

"You don't go there for the clubs, do you?"

"Well, no. But there won't be much to do."

"Can you see the stars? You can't see them in the city."

Lucas thought of the big telescope in the great room. He'd bought it even before he'd bought furniture.

"Yeah. You can."

"And crickets. Can you hear them at night?"

Her tone was wistful. He looked at her and cleared his throat again.

"After sundown, it's a cricket symphony."

She turned her face to him. "I grew up in the country."

He felt a twinge of guilt because he already knew that.

"And I love the city. The energy, the endless wonderful places to explore… But there are some things about the country I'll always miss. The quiet." She smiled. "The stars. And the sound of crickets." She gave a little laugh. "Sounds silly, I suppose, but—"

To hell with traffic.

Lucas checked the mirrors, shot across a lane of traffic

to the blare of angry horns and pulled to the curb. He undid his seat belt, undid Caroline's, gathered her in his arms and kissed her.

They were almost at his beach house when Caroline gasped and said, "Oh my gosh. Oliver!"

Lucas nodded. Oliver, indeed. The cat had food, water and the attitude of a lion. He suspected Oliver could take care of himself for a day, but he didn't say that. Instead, he called Mrs. Kennelly on his cell, apologized for the intrusion and asked if she could stop by to deal with Oliver.

"I know I told you to take the week off and this is lot to ask…"

"I'll do better than that, sir," his housekeeper said. "I'll stay with him."

"Oh, you don't have to do—"

"I'm happy to do it. Oliver's such a fine, sweet-natured cat!"

Sweet-natured? Lucas said that was good to hear.

"Okay," he said, when he ended the call. "Mrs. Kennelly will stay with Oliver."

"Thank you."

Lucas reached for Caroline's hand. And felt a tightness in his chest. The house was down the next lane. Would she like it?

"We're here," he said.

Caroline sat up straight. Ahead, she saw massive stone walls and impressive iron gates. Lucas pressed a button, the gates swung open and she caught her breath.

She wasn't naive. She'd lived in New York long enough to know that property in the Hamptons was expensive but the sight of Lucas's so-called beach house took her breath away.

Glass, he'd said. And a deck, and a pool. What he hadn't

mentioned was that there were what looked like acres of glass, or that the deck seemed to hang over a beach that stretched over the dunes to the sea, or that a waterfall tumbled into the pool, or that the pool was the kind that seemed to have no boundaries around it.

"It's called an infinity pool," Lucas said as he took her on a slow walk around the place.

"It's wonderful. All of it. Wonderful," Caroline said, beaming up at him.

He nodded. "Yes," he said, as if it didn't matter, because it mattered too much, "it's nice."

"Nice?" She laughed, let go of his hand and danced out in front of him. "It's incredible!"

What was incredible, he thought, was the color in Caroline's face, the glow in her eyes. Watching her brought back the excitement he'd felt helping design the house, explaining what he wanted to the architect and builders.

When they stepped through the front door, she gave a soft, breathless "oooh" of delight.

High ceilings. Skylights. White walls. Italian tile floors in some rooms, bamboo in others.

"It's like a dream," she said softly. "It's perfect!"

"Perfect," Lucas said, and he drew her into his arms.

"What's the rest of it like?"

He smiled. "I'll show you." Slowly, he eased the hoodie from her shoulders. "I'll show you all of it. But now—" He swung her into his arms. "Let me show you the master bedroom," he said softly.

Caroline looped her arms around his neck and buried her face against his throat.

"That's an excellent idea," she said, and thought, *if this is a dream, may it never end.*

* * *

They did all the things he'd imagined doing here but had somehow never done.

They made love. Went skinny-dipping in the heated pool after he assured Caroline there were no neighbors; his property extended for more than five acres around and behind the house. He found an old shirt for her to wear; he put on shorts and they poked around in the kitchen cupboards and the freezer to find stuff for lunch.

At sunset, they strolled along the beach, just at the surfline, the cool Atlantic nipping at their toes. Drove into town, to a quiet little café for a candlelit dinner. When they returned to the house, the sky was deepest black and the stars blazed fiercely overhead.

"The stars," Caroline said in a hushed voice.

They watched the heavens from the deck, her leaning back against Lucas, his arms hard around her.

Lucas could feel her heart beating. He could hear the soft whisper of her breath.

Something inside him seemed to rise and take flight.

He was happy.

"Caroline," he whispered.

He turned her in his arms. She looked up at him, her face pale and lovely in the light of a full moon.

"Caroline," he said again, and because he knew there was more to say and that he was afraid to say it, he bent his head and kissed her.

Then he undressed her.

Eased her out of her clothing with the moon and the stars looking on. Stripped her bare and shuddered when she reached to him and began undressing him, too.

When they were naked, he led her inside, to his bedroom, to an enormous bed on a platform under a huge skylight that let in the burning light of the sky.

Lucas worshipped her mouth. Her breasts. Her dusty-rose

nipples. He kissed her belly, her thighs, moved between them and stroked her hot, ready flesh with the tips of his fingers.

"Watch me as I make love to you," he said thickly, and Caroline wanted to tell him she would watch him forever, that she adored him, that she loved him, loved him, loved him...

And then he was deep inside her and the world went away.

They drove into town the next day, to a little shop on Jobs Lane so simple on the outside that Caroline knew, instinctively, she could never afford anything it sold, but she needed a change of clothes.

Lucas wanted to buy her everything he saw. She said an emphatic "no," selected a bra, panties, a cotton sweater and a pair of cropped pants.

"I'll pay you back," she whispered after the clerk had gone in back to wrap them.

He laughed, twiddled an imaginary mustache, bent her back over his arm, gave her a dramatic kiss and said yes, she surely would.

She laughed, too. She knew he was joking, that he would never let her give him the hundreds of dollars the handful of items had cost and it was a sudden jolt of reality, a reminder that there was very little money left in her bank account, that she had to find a job, and quickly.

And she had to find a place to live.

The realization made her unusually quiet on the trip back to the beach house. How had she let herself become so dependent on this man? She thought of her mother and shuddered.

"*Querida?* Shall I put on the heat?"

"No," she said quickly, forcing a smile as she turned toward him. "I'm fine. Just—maybe too much sun this afternoon, hmm? What do you think?"

"I think," he said solemnly, reaching for her hand and

lifting it to his lips, "I think that there is only one way to deal with a chill."

How could she not laugh? She did, and Lucas looked at her and grinned. He loved that laugh of hers. It was sexy, earthy, and yet, somehow, innocent.

"You do, huh?"

"*Sim*," he said, and proved it to her as soon as they reached the house.

They stayed at the beach for two days.

Lucas would have stayed for the rest of the week but his P.A. called on his cell phone, filled with apologies, to tell him that the owner and CEO of a French bank he'd been looking at for months had phoned and asked for a meeting.

"I wouldn't have bothered you, Mr. Vieira, but—"

Lucas assured her she'd been right to call. Still, when he told Caroline it was time to return to the city, he couldn't help feeling that something irreplaceable was coming to an end.

She seemed to sense the same thing. She stepped into his arms and cuddled against him while he stroked her hair.

"Ah," she said with a sad little smile, "what's that old saying? All good things must come to an end."

She spoke the words lightly but Lucas felt a chill.

"We'll come back on the weekend," he said. "I promise."

But they didn't come back on the weekend. He should have known they wouldn't.

He should have known that she'd gotten it right.

All good things always did come to an end.

# CHAPTER ELEVEN

THERE came a time when a person could no longer evade reality.

It had happened to Lucas as a boy, the day his mother abandoned him.

Now, it was happening again. Returning to the city was like taking an icy plunge into the real world. No more starry nights, no more crickets, no more lingering over a bottle of wine before dinner on the deck overlooking the sea.

They drove to New York early the next morning. By noon, life had returned to what Lucas had, for many years, thought of as normal.

He was in his office, dressed in banker's gray Armani, meeting with his staff and planning the strategy of the next three days, which was how long the French banker would be in the city.

Someone had done a quick PowerPoint presentation. Someone else had run pages and pages of numbers. His team was sharp, intelligent, hand-picked.

But he found it difficult to concentrate.

His thoughts kept circling back to the days and nights in the Hamptons and to the perfect little world he and Caroline had created.

Leaving her this morning had been one of the hardest things he'd ever done.

"I'll call you when I can," he'd said, as he held her in his arms.

She'd fussed with his tie, smoothed back his dark hair and smiled up at him.

"I'll miss you," she'd said softly.

"No," he'd said with a quick smile, "you won't. You have all those boxes from your office to go through."

"I'll miss you," Caroline had said again, and Lucas's smile had faded. He would miss her, too. Terribly. How could a woman have won his—have won his interest so completely in only a handful of days?

"I'll get rid of the Frenchman in no time."

"You can't do that, Lucas. I don't want you to do that. I'm not going to keep you from your responsibilities."

*You're my responsibility*, he thought…and the realization that he wanted her to be his responsibility had stunned him.

"What?" Caroline had said, reading something in his eyes.

"Nothing." *Everything.* But he wasn't ready to think about what that meant. Not yet. Instead, he'd raised her face to his and kissed her. "We'll go somewhere special for dinner. How's that sound?"

"Anyplace would be special with you," she'd replied, and his heart felt as if it might take wing.

Now, with the hours passing, he knew he wouldn't get rid of the French banker all that quickly. He probably wouldn't even make it home for dinner, let alone in time to take Caroline somewhere special.

The Frenchman was eager to conclude a deal he'd been sitting on for months and Lucas was, too. The quicker, the better.

Then he could get back to more important things.

To Caroline.

He phoned her a few times during the day. The phone rang

and rang and then, with Mrs. Kennelly gone again, went to voice mail.

"Hi," he said whenever it did, "it's me."

He said that he missed her. That he was sorry but he wouldn't be home in time for dinner. He said he'd only just realized he had never taken her cell number and would she call him when she had the chance and give it to him.

She didn't call.

And he began to worry.

Foolish, he knew. She was capable of taking care of herself and she was not new to the city, but he worried anyway. Had she gone back to her apartment? Was she there even now, in that run-down building, that dangerous street with a dangerous burglar on the loose? He couldn't think of a reason she would be, but he knew how stubbornly independent she was.

So he worried, and it was a new experience. Worrying about someone. About a woman. Thinking about her, all the time.

It made him edgy.

He felt as if he were at some kind of turning point. Caroline dominated his thoughts. He had—he had feelings for her that transcended even what he felt for her in bed.

In midafternoon, after an endless lunch with the Frenchman, Lucas went back to his office, checked his cell phone for messages on the way, his desk phone for voice mail when he got there. He ran his hand through his hair, told himself to stop being an idiot…

And went out of his office, to his P.A.'s desk.

"Has a Ms. Hamilton phoned?"

"No, sir," she said politely, but he saw the curiosity in her eyes. Her phone rang while he was standing there. "Lucas Vieira's office," she said, listened, looked at Lucas who was already reaching for the receiver. She muted the call and shook her head. "It's a Realtor for you, sir."

A Realtor? Lucas nodded, went into his office and took the call. He'd damned near forgotten asking the guy to find an apartment for Caroline.

"Vieira here," he said briskly.

The Realtor's voice bubbled with good news. He'd found the perfect place. On Park Avenue. A building with a doorman, of course. Concierge service. Within an easy walk of Lucas's penthouse on Fifth. Three big rooms. A fireplace. A terrace. The keys were with the doorman, if Lucas wanted to take a look.

Lucas swiveled his chair around, massaged his forehead with the tips of his fingers.

"Yes," he said, "it sounds fine. But—"

But what?

But, he didn't want to think about Caroline living apart from him. Didn't want to imagine waking in the morning without her in his arms, or going to sleep at night without her head on his shoulder.

He told the Realtor he'd get back to him.

Told himself that he needed to think.

Caroline couldn't stay with him indefinitely. Of course, she couldn't. He didn't do that. He never had. He'd never had a woman living with him before. Not that a handful of days qualified as someone living with him but it was a serious change in the pattern he'd always maintained.

His mistresses always had their own places; he'd paid the rent for more than a few of them. And he'd never given any thought to doing things another way.

Live with a woman under his roof? Be with her 24/7? Wake up with her. Go to sleep with her. Start the entire thing over again the following morning?

The idea had always seemed impossible.

Now, it seemed—it seemed not just possible but, but interesting. Even enticing.

He reached for the phone, tried his penthouse again. *Ring. Ring. Ring.* And then, Caroline, sounding breathless, said, "Hello?"

*"Querida."* Lucas expelled a sigh of relief. "I was worried about you."

Caroline smiled. It was lovely to hear those words from her lover. It made her feel cherished.

"Why would you worry? I'm fine."

"I know. I was just being—just overly cautious, I guess." He wanted to ask if she'd gone to her apartment but decided against it. He had no right to check up on her. "Did you have a good day?"

Caroline looked at the little gaily wrapped package in her hand. It was from Barnes and Noble. Inside the wrapping was a book about the stars and the planets. They'd used Lucas's telescope one night at his beach house and argued over which group of stars was the constellation Cassiopeia and which wasn't.

The argument had ended in the way all arguments should, she thought now, loving the memory of Lucas sweeping her off her feet and into his arms.

"There's only one way to settle this," he'd said with a mock growl, and she'd squealed in equally fake indignation as he took her to his bed.

The book was to be a surprise.

She wanted badly to give him something, a gift from her that would have meaning, but the gorgeous Steuben glass sculptures, the Winslow Homer prints of ships and the sea that she'd spent the afternoon looking at were thousands of times beyond her means.

The book would be just right.

It wasn't an expensive gift, especially not for a man like him, but she'd learned enough about Lucas to know that what she'd paid for it wouldn't matter. He'd love the book because he loved looking at the stars.

And maybe he'd love it even more because it was from her.

Not that she was foolish enough to think he'd fallen in love with her but he did care for her, she was certain of that.

He'd even stopped looking at her as he had every once in a while at the beginning, an expression on his face that she couldn't read but that had frightened her just the same. It was as if he didn't approve of her, as if he were judging her, and whenever it had happened, she'd come close to asking him what he was thinking. But then that look would vanish, and why would she ask questions that might bring it back?

"Sweetheart? Are you still there?"

"Yes," Caroline said, "I'm here."

"I know I said I'd be home for dinner, but—"

"That's all right," she said, even though it wasn't. She missed him terribly. "I understand."

"Good." Not good. He'd wanted her to tell him she was devastated by the news.

"I'm liable to be very late, so if you get tired, don't wait up for me. *Sim*?"

"*Sim*," Caroline said softly.

But when he came home just before midnight, she was waiting in the living room, Oliver in her lap, and the minute he stepped from the elevator she put the cat aside and ran straight into Lucas's arms.

"I missed you," she said, and as he held her to his heart, he knew he wasn't going to sign the lease on that apartment for her.

He wasn't ready to let her go.

And in the very back of his mind, he began to wonder if he ever would be.

* * *

He rose at six the next morning, showered, dressed, dropped a light kiss on Caroline's hair as she slept and headed to the kitchen for a cup of coffee.

He'd told his staff to be prepared to work through the weekend. They understood. The deal was important. What they couldn't possibly know was that Lucas wanted to conclude it so he could clear his agenda for the next couple of weeks. He hadn't been to his Caribbean island since he'd bought it. He wanted to go there with Caroline. She'd love it. The privacy, the sea...

"Good morning."

He turned and saw her in the doorway, yawning, her hair in her eyes, barefoot, wearing one of his T-shirts and he thought, *No way in the world am I going to work today.*

He told her that as he poured coffee for them both and sat down beside her at the white stone counter. She shook her head.

"Of course you are," she said.

"Hey," he said, flashing her a supposedly indignant smile, "I'm the boss, remember?"

"Exactly. You're the boss. People depend on you." She fluttered her lashes and leaned toward him. "I should have known I'd be too ravishing a sight for you to deal with at this hour of the day."

She laughed but he didn't. She *was* ravishing, uncombed hair, no makeup, the tiniest fold in her cheek from sleeping with her head on his shoulder.

*I love you*, he thought, and the realization swept through him with the unbridled force of a tidal wave.

"Caroline," he said, "Caroline..."

No. This wasn't the moment. He'd wait until tonight, when he wasn't about to rush out the door. He'd take her someplace romantic and quiet. Candles, music, the whole sentimental thing he'd always thought foolish, and he'd put his heart in her hands.

It was a terrifying prospect but—but she cared for him. He could tell. Hell, she loved him. She had to love him...

"Lucas?" She put her hand over his. "What's the matter?"

"Nothing. I, uh, I just—I just— You know, you never gave me your cell number."

She held out her hand. He was baffled for a moment. Then he dug his cell from his pocket and gave it to her. She punched in numbers, made the entry and handed it back.

"Just don't worry if you can't reach me," she said. "I'm going job-hunting. And apartment hunting. Well, I won't try to do both today, but—"

"You don't need to do either."

Her heart skipped a beat. What did that mean? What was he thinking? About her? About their situation? Anything was possible, she thought, anything.

Even a miracle.

"You have a place to live," he said gruffly. "And if you need money..."

He took our his wallet, pulled out a sheaf of bills.

So much for miracles.

"Do not," Caroline said with sudden coldness, "do not do that."

"But if you need money—"

"I know how to earn it."

He looked at her. The uptilted chin. The defiant set to her mouth. The determined glint in her hazel eyes.

And for one awful instant, he thought, *How?*

He hated himself for it.

He had been wrong about her from Day One. She'd never taken money for sex. He'd finally come to believe it. She was incredible in bed but that was only because there was something special between them. She was innately passionate; he'd just been the man lucky enough to find that passion in her and set it free.

Why should such an ugly thought even cross his mind now?

"I almost forgot," he said, trying to lighten the moment. "The Queen of the Greasy Spoon."

She didn't move. Didn't change that look on her face. Then, finally, she nodded.

"That's me," she said, but he could still hear the tension in her voice. He wanted to tell her she wouldn't need a job or a place to live, not after tonight when he told her he wanted her to stay with him. To be with him. To be—to be—

His head was swimming. There was too much going on. The French deal. And now this.

Tonight. There'd be time to talk tonight. To figure things out. For now, he murmured her name and took her in his arms. After a minute, the tension went out of her; she leaned into him, sighed and put her arms around his neck.

"Sweetheart. *Querida*, I just want you to be happy."

"I am happy," she said softly.

She walked him to the elevator. He tilted her face to his and kissed her. But as the elevator took him away from her, Caroline wrapped her arms around herself to ward off a sudden chill.

*I am not my mother*, she thought fiercely. And Lucas was not like any of the men who'd used her mother so badly.

But the ugly image—Lucas, pulling that money from his pocket—lingered. And, without warning, she thought again of the way he'd looked at her every once in a while, at the start of their relationship.

She almost pressed the elevator button and went after him. But she wasn't dressed. Besides, she was being foolish.

Something soft pressed against her ankle. It was Oliver, purring like a small engine.

"Foolish," Caroline said softly, and she lifted the cat into her arms.

It was a typical New York-in-June day. Cool in the morning, warm in the afternoon, hot by the time Caroline had trudged from restaurant to diner to deli.

With zero success.

Nobody needed a waitress.

College and high school kids seemed to have snapped up all the openings. There was one possibility, in a deli near Union Square, but the manager had put his hand on her butt as she was leaving and she knew it would not stop with that, so she'd scratched the place off her list.

This time of year, the odds on a translating job were slim to none. Still, she stopped on campus anyway on the odd chance something might be available. There was, not translating, just some research on Pushkin, but the prof who needed it wouldn't be in until the next day.

Her cell phone buzzed a couple of times. Lucas, saying he just wanted to hear her voice, which went a long way toward making her feel better.

Still, she returned home—to Lucas's home—sweaty and weary. The doorman greeted her by name; the concierge, too. It felt nice, having them know her.

But she could not, must not, get used to it.

Oliver gave her his usual big greeting. Caroline picked him up, kissed his scarred head and told him what a good boy he was. She put him down, went into the kitchen, put ice in a glass, filled it with water...

Her cell phone rang.

Not Lucas. It was Dani Sinclair. Surprised, Caroline took the call.

Dani cut right to the chase.

"I have a translating job I can't do," she said briskly. "Tomorrow, four in the afternoon at the Roosevelt Hotel. It shouldn't take you more than a couple of hours. Interested?"

Caroline sat at the counter.

"I won't do anything like what I did last time, Dani. No pretending to be someone I'm not."

Dani chuckled. "Relax, sweetie. This is a straight deal. A Russian bigwig has a suite there, he's meeting with a guy representing the mayor's office. The mayor's rep will have his own translator. The Russian wants one, too. He called me because I've worked for him before but, you know, I have another engagement. What do you say?"

Despite Dani's assurances, Caroline still hesitated. The night she'd spent standing in for the other woman had left her with mixed feelings. It had led her to meeting Lucas, and that was wonderful, but the evening had had a strangeness to it she couldn't get past.

"Listen, you can't tell me you don't need the work. There's nothing much out there. You know how it is when the university's on summer session."

"You're right," Caroline said slowly. Oliver meowed and jumped into her lap. "But I might have something tomorrow."

"At school?"

"Yes. With Ethan Brustein."

"Yuck."

Caroline laughed. Professor Brustein was not well-liked. He was brilliant, but he had a nasty temper and a short fuse.

"I know. Brustein's not my idea of a good time, either, but he only wants an hour or two with me."

"The job at the hotel is three hours, minimum. Might run to four."

"Four hours," Caroline said slowly. "And I'll only have to handle the one guy?"

"Didn't I just say that?" Dani said impatiently.

"Well… Okay. Give me his name and his suite number. Oh, and how much is he supposed to pay me, and—"

*"Mrroww!"*

Oliver jumped to the floor, using Caroline's thigh as a springboard. Tail bushed, back arched, he stood at her feet, hissing. Caroline swung around and saw Lucas, standing in the doorway.

All her weariness vanished. She got to her feet, her lips curving in a smile.

"Lucas. What a nice sur—"

She stopped in midsentence. Lucas's face was dark. Stony. His green eyes were the color of the winter sea.

Her heart gave a resounding thump.

"Dani," she said into the phone, "I have to go."

"No, wait. I didn't give you the guy's name and—"

"I'll call you back," Caroline said, and flipped her phone shut. "Lucas? What's wrong?"

His lips drew back from his teeth in a chilling parody of a smile.

"Why should anything be wrong?"

"I don't know. That's why I asked the question." Her eyes swept over him. There it was again, that cold, accusative expression. No. This was worse. His posture was rigid, his hands were knotted at his sides. "Sweetheart. Please. What's happened?"

Lucas felt as if he were drowning in rage.

It was the first time she'd used a term of endearment instead of his name. It should have filled him with happiness. Instead, it added to his fury. How could she call him "sweetheart" after what he'd just heard? That brisk business chat with Dani Sinclair. About Caroline's return to—to work.

Bile rose in his throat.

She was standing in front of him now, staring at him through enormous eyes. She wore sandals, a pink cotton tank top and a white cotton skirt; there was a little white purse still slung across her body.

She'd obviously just come home. The doorman had told him so and he'd ridden the elevator filled with a hot combination of joy and terror at what he was about to do, to say, stepped out of it and heard her voice, followed it here, saw her looking beautiful and sweetly innocent…

Maybe that was her particular forté. That look of girlish innocence. That supposed naiveté. It had worked on him before.

But it would never work on him again.

"Lucas?"

She put her hand on his arm. He shook it off.

"I told you, nothing happened. Nothing's wrong. I came back early, that's all."

Caroline stared at him. Of course, something was wrong. Very wrong, and whatever it was, it had to do with her. She swallowed, moistened her lips with the tip of her tongue.

"I'm—I'm happy that you did."

More words to torment him. He thought of how he'd suddenly lost all interest in the contract he and the Frenchman had been discussing, how he'd shot to his feet during drinks with the man.

The banker had looked as surprised as Lucas had felt.

And then, maybe because the banker was French and the French were supposed to know about affairs of the heart, or maybe because he just couldn't keep from doing what he knew he had to do, he'd said that there was a woman, that he was sorry, that he had to leave.

The banker had smiled, risen from his chair and held out his hand.

"What is it you Americans say? Go for it, dude!"

Lucas had laughed, rushed out the door, snared a taxi, told the driver there was an extra fifty in the tip if he got him home in record time...

"Lucas. Please. Talk to me. What are you thinking? Why are you looking at me that way?"

His jaw tightened. *Slow down*, a voice within him said, *damnit, man, slow down and think.*

But he couldn't.

He felt as if he were dying and the only way to stop that from happening was to keep moving and do what he should have done right from the beginning.

Get Caroline Hamilton out of his life.

Or put her into it, but in the only way they'd both understand.

He told her to follow him.

"Follow him" turned out to be exactly what he meant.

His pace was breakneck. Into the elevator. Down to the lobby. Through it, without pause. No *hello, how are you, nice day* formalities to the concierge or the doorman, no lessening of his stride as he went out the door and started briskly toward the corner.

Caroline had to trot to keep up.

"Where are we going?" she said, but he didn't answer and finally she gave up, concentrated on trying to stay with him as they crossed Madison Avenue and approached Park where Lucas made his way to a tall apartment building. A few words to the doorman, then a key changed hands.

"Shall I send someone up with you, sir?" the doorman said.

Lucas didn't bother answering. He put his hand in the small of Caroline's back and damned near pushed her into the lobby, then into the elevator.

Her heart wasn't just thumping, it was threatening to burst from her chest.

"Lucas." Her voice shook. "Lucas, what is this about?"

Still no answer.

The elevator stopped. The doors opened. Lucas got out. Caroline told herself to stand her ground. Why should she follow him when he wouldn't tell her where they were going? When he wouldn't speak a single word? But curiosity and a simmering anger got the better of her, and she did.

Down the hall. Past two doors. Three. He came to a halt. She watched as he took a deep breath, then stabbed the key into the lock. The door swung open on a tiled foyer that opened onto a handsome living room. She saw a terrace. A fireplace. A view of Park Avenue.

Lucas's eyes were cold and flat as he motioned her forward and let the door swing shut behind her. She turned and looked at him. She could hear the beat of her heart throbbing in her ears.

"What is this place?"

"It's your new home, *querida*. Three rooms, complete with a view."

"I don't—I don't understand—"

"You can select your own furnishings. Or call ABC. Or Bloomingdale's. Let a designer handle things."

"I don't understand," she said again, but in a voice so small, so pathetic it didn't sound like her own because, of course, all at once, she did.

"I've already ordered some clothes for you. From Saks. They'll deliver whenever you—"

"I don't want any of this. Why would you even think I would?"

"The apartment is in my name. You'll charge the furniture to me, as well. I'll open accounts for you at whatever shops you like."

"Lucas!" She stepped in front of him, looked up at his stony face. She was shaking; her legs felt as if the muscles were turning to water. "Don't do this. I beg you. Don't—"

"In addition, I'll deposit forty thousand a month into whatever bank you choose."

Caroline's hand flew to her mouth. Her head was spinning. She was going to faint. Or be sick.

"Not enough? Fifty, then." Lucas reached for her hand, folded her lifeless fingers around the key. "With only one stipulation."

She gasped as he caught her wrists, hoisted her to her toes. His mouth came down on hers, hard and hurtful.

"You'll belong to me," he growled, "for as long as I want you. Nobody else. No other men. No arrangements through Dani Sinclair or some other procurer." His mouth twisted. "I don't want the smell, the taste of anyone else on you. Just me, you understand? Only me, until I'm tired of—"

Caroline wrenched away, tears streaming down her face.

"I hate you," she said, "I hate you, I hate you, I hate—"

An agonized cry broke from her throat. She whirled toward the door. Flung it open. Lucas reached out for her, then let his hand fall to his side.

The elevator swallowed her up. He was alone.

Nothing new in that. He had always been alone.

But never as much as in that last, terrible moment.

# CHAPTER TWELVE

Dusk had finally faded to the cheerless dark of night.

A black, impenetrable night.

No moon. No stars. Nothing but the mournful sigh of the wind, swooping through the maze of Manhattan's concrete canyons in advance of a predicted rainstorm.

Lucas sat in his living room, a glass of Scotch between his palms. The room was dark. Not even the glow of the street lamps in Central Park, the distant lights of the city skyline, could penetrate the massing clouds.

Any minute now, he'd turn on the lamps, head into the kitchen and heat something for his dinner. He just wasn't hungry yet. Wasn't in the mood for lights, either.

The cry of the wind, the advancing storm, the all-encompassing darkness, suited his mood.

It was hard to accept you'd been played for a fool by a pretty face and a soft voice. And, damnit, it had happened to him twice in as many weeks. First Elin, now Caroline.

Lucas lifted the glass to his lips, took a long swallow.

No.

This was a night for honesty. What had happened with Elin had been little more than a petty annoyance. What had happened with Caroline was…

It was different.

For a little while, he'd thought she was—that she might

be—that there was something more than sex between them. He gave a bitter laugh.

And there had been.

There'd been her, reeling him in like a trout on a line.

"Stupid," he growled, "damned stupid fool!"

How had he let it happen? He, of all men. He'd grown up knowing what the world was like. No teddy bears and fairy tales for him. The world took. It never gave. You survived only by never forgetting that hard-won wisdom.

As for women— Another lesson learned in childhood. At his mother's knee, you might say. Women lied. They cheated. They said they loved you and then—

"Hell," he said, and drank more of the Scotch. No point in going overboard. Caroline had never said she loved him. And he, thank God, had never said he loved her.

A damned good thing, because he hadn't. He'd let himself toy with the idea, that was all.

Amazing, what a few days and nights of particularly good sex could do to a man's mind but then, a woman like Caroline would be good at sex. She'd make it an art.

And he couldn't even place all the blame on her. After all, he'd known what she was from the start. He'd just convinced himself that he had it wrong. The sighs. The whispers. The incredibly innocent, incredibly arousing ways she'd touched him, explored his body as if sex, as if men, as it everything they did when she was in his arms was new…

"Back to square one," he muttered.

She hadn't been naive. He was the one. He'd been more than naive. He'd been a fool.

Lucas drained the last of the whisky, rose to his feet and went to the sideboard where he'd left the bottle of Macallan. He poured another generous couple of inches, then drank.

Now he was compounding his stupid actions by feeling sorry for himself. Well, no way was he going to continue with that. It was unproductive. Unmanly. The thing to do was get past his anger, put what had happened in perspective.

And if that meant getting the memory of Caroline out of his head, the taste of her off his lips, so be it. When a man lived with a woman, memories of her were bound to linger.

Except, he hadn't lived with Caroline. A week didn't constitute "living with" anyone.

But he'd come painfully close to asking her to do just that. Live with him. Stay with him. Be his—his mistress. Only his mistress; he'd never have wanted her to be more than that…

And wasn't that a laugh? What was it she'd said, back when they'd met? Something about not believing in women being mistresses? Oh, yeah, she'd been good at games.

Another long drink of whisky. Maybe enough of it would thaw the lump of ice that seemed lodged in his heart.

If he'd come home five minutes sooner. Or five minutes later. Or if he hadn't been so quiet as he stepped out of the elevator, he'd never have heard that conversation.

But he'd wanted to surprise her with a declaration of—of what? Not love. *Caralho*, not that! The most he'd have said was *Caroline, will you live with me? Will you stay here with me because I—because I—*

Lucas shuddered.

Why in hell had she been making that—that appointment through the Sinclair woman? Money? He'd tried to give her some only this morning and look how that had turned out. And that time in Southampton, when he'd taken her shopping on Jobs Lane… He'd have bought out the boutique but she'd refused to let him buy anything but the simple things she absolutely needed.

It just didn't make sense.

Unless she'd been scheming for the bigger prize. Waiting and hoping he'd actually ask her to become his wife.

No. She must have known he'd never have done that.

His mistress, then. That would have been a coup. Trouble with that theory was that, basically, he'd made that offer at the Park Avenue apartment. He hadn't done it romantically but surely he'd offered her everything a woman like her could want. An expensive flat. Charge cards. A monthly stipend. Wasn't all that a fair enough substitute for hearts and flowers?

Apparently not—which left only one other possibility.

What she'd wanted from the deal she'd been making through Dani Sinclair was sex.

Sex with somebody else. With a different man. A different man than him.

A new face. A new body. Someone else's hands on her. Someone else's mouth. Rougher sex, maybe, but, goddamnit, if she wanted it rough...

Lucas hurled the glass of Scotch at the wall. The amber liquid darkened the ivory surface; shards of glass rained down on the floor.

Who gave a damn?

The cat would. If it walked on the bits of glass. Not that he gave a damn about the cat but the animal was his responsibility. For now, anyway. Tomorrow, he'd call the ASPCA.

His mouth twisted as he went to the utility closet.

Caroline had walked out on the cat, same as she'd walked out on him. And she *had* walked out on him, never mind the part he'd played.

Glass swept, wall sponged, he put everything away, glanced at the illuminated dial of his watch.

Tomorrow was Sunday but he had meetings scheduled throughout the day. His staff at eight. His attorneys at nine, his CFO and his accountants at ten. And, finally, the French banker at noon. He needed to be sharp. Alert. All this nonsense gone and forgotten. And it would be.

Damned right, it would be.

One last glass of whisky before bed…

Lightning slashed the sky; thunder roared. The storm was finally here. Good, he thought as he settled into a corner of the living room sofa. Storms, summer storms especially, always left the city seeming fresh and new.

That was how he would feel in the morning. As if he were starting over. No more thoughts of Caroline, or trying to figure out what he'd felt for her. What he'd *imagined* he'd felt for her. No more wondering how he could have fallen for that sweet and innocent act, for believing she'd cared for him.

Lucas snorted. What she'd cared about was delivering a stellar performance, starting with the masquerade that first night with the Rostovs.

Lightning lit the room again. Thunder rolled overhead, loud enough, near enough to make the whisky in the glass shiver.

Something brushed against his ankle. Lucas jerked back.

*"Meow?"*

It was the cat. The big, ugly, vile-tempered cat Caroline had professed to love.

Lucas glared at the creature. "What the hell do you want?"

*"Mrrorw,"* the cat said, and this time, when lightning flashed through the room, Lucas saw that the animal was shaking.

"Don't tell me you're scared. A take-no-prisoners tough guy like you?"

The cat leaned against Lucas's leg. He could feel it trembling.

He watched the cat for a long minute. Then he put his glass on the coffee table and offered his hand, fingers outstretched, for sniffing.

"Bite me," he said, "and you'll never see a bowl of Daintee Deelites again."

The cat made a small, questioning sound. Carefully, in

what looked like slow motion, it leaned forward and pressed its battered head, face first, into Lucas's palm.

This was not fair.

Lucas was not a cat person.

The cat was not a Lucas-person.

Over the last week, they'd developed a gentleman's understanding. Lucas had tolerated the cat's presence. The cat had tolerated his. Caroline had been their go-between and yes, she was gone but the cat still had food, water and shelter.

What more could a street cat possibly want?

*"Mrrow, mrrow, mrrow,"* the cat said in a voice that would better have suited a purebred Persian.

Lucas scowled.

"Damnit," he said, and lifted the cat into his arms. "I'm not her, okay? I don't do cuddling. And soothing. You want any of that, you've got the wrong guy."

The cat settled like a warm pillow against his chest, looked into his face, gave a meow so soft and sweet it had no business coming from The Cat from Hell.

A muscle knotted in Lucas's jaw.

*"Sim,"* he said gruffly, "I know. She's gone. And you miss her."

He swallowed hard. Stroked his big hand over the cat's—over Oliver's—beat-up ears.

"Damnit," he whispered, "so do I."

Oliver offered another plaintive little *meow*, raised his head and rubbed it against Lucas's jaw.

Lucas closed his eyes. He felt moisture on his cheeks, tasted salt on his lips.

Did cats cry?

They must, for surely these tears could not be his.

Caroline had spent the past hours hot with rage.

She knew that her anger was all but written across her face.

She probably looked like a deranged street person. New Yorkers, inured to the odd, the unusual and, therefore, the dangerous, kept their distance, edging away from her on the subway, giving her a wide berth on the walk from the station to her old apartment house. A drunk or a doper, whatever he was, said "whoa" and scurried away as she ran up the stairs to the front door.

Good. Excellent.

Nobody was going to screw around with her and get away with it.

Caroline unlocked her apartment door, set the locks, threw her purse on the sagging sofa and began pacing from one end of the shoebox-size living room to the other.

That rat! That no-good, cold-blooded, arrogant, self-centered, self-aggrandizing... And if she was repeating herself, so be it.

"How could you?" she said. "Damn you to hell, Lucas Vieira, how *could* you?"

That awful, horrible, ugly thing he'd said. About her. About not wanting to—to smell other men on her, to taste them on her, the brutal, obvious implication being that she—that she would ever—that she was a woman who would—

"Bastard," she snarled, and kicked the sofa as she marched by.

And that look on his face. That look she'd seen on it before. That look she'd never understood. She understood it now. He'd always thought of her as—as a whore. Because that was what it came down to, didn't it? That a man who'd say such things to a woman thought that woman was—that she was little better than—than—

A sob rose in her throat. But she would not cry. She would not! Lucas didn't deserve her tears.

He was cold. He was evil. He was insane. How else to explain that after all he'd said, he'd added that he wanted her to be his mistress? He'd all but commanded it. She was to live in a place he'd paid for, wear clothes he bought her, spend money he deposited in a bank account for her so that he could have her near enough to—to use when the mood was on him.

This time, she couldn't keep a low, agonized sob from bursting from her lips.

"Stop that," she said fiercely.

What was there to cry about? She was angry, not sorrowful. She was better off without him. A thousand times better off. She just could not understand how a man who'd seemed so tender and caring could have turned into a monster right before her eyes.

Caroline flung herself down on the sofa. Snatched a throw pillow and wrapped her arms around it.

"I hate you, Lucas!"

Her voice shook but it was only with anger. Anger was what she felt, she reminded herself. It was all she felt. Why would she feel anything else, ever, for him?

What made it even worse was that she knew, in her heart, that she had to shoulder some of the blame.

She'd slept with him the first night they met. What kind of woman did that? Lots, she knew, but not someone like her.

Then, a couple of days later, she'd moved into his home. Into his bed. Let him pay for the roof over her head, the food that went into her belly. Let him take her away for what she'd thought of as a magical, impromptu weekend when he'd probably had it all planned.

He'd figured he was buying her. That she was a woman a man *could* buy...

The years she'd spent, condemning her mother's behavior, thinking of Mama as stupid for trusting men, for giving away her heart. The years she'd spent, telling herself she'd never, ever be as foolish as that.

Caroline swallowed hard.

And here she was—surprise, surprise—a proverbial chip off the old block, a foolish woman walking right in her mother's footsteps.

Caroline jumped to her feet. Enough. No way was she succumbing to self-pity!

God, the apartment was stifling! The only window in the living room was the one at the fire escape and now there was an iron gate across it. She could still open the window but the thought of it being open, gate or no gate, made her feel sick.

Water, splashed on her face and wrists would cool her off. An old trick, but sometimes it worked.

She went into the tiny bathroom, switched on the light and stared at herself in the mirror over the sink. A creature with disheveled hair and a red, blotchy face stared back.

"Pitiful," Caroline said, "absolutely pitiful, thinking that man cared for you. Thinking you cared for him. Because you didn't. You didn't. You—"

Her voice broke.

Quickly, she turned on the cold water, scooped some up and splashed it over her burning cheeks.

Lucas meant nothing to her.

Oliver did.

Tomorrow was Sunday, but Lucas would be going to his office. He'd told her so, even sounded apologetic about it. Well, as soon as she knew he'd left, she'd go collect the cat. She hated leaving him alone at Lucas's tonight…

Lucas wouldn't turn him out, would he?

No. The man obviously had a block of ice where he was supposed to have a heart but even he wouldn't do a thing like that.

Caroline reached for a towel, dried her face and hands.

It was time to make plans.

She'd get Oliver. And her things. Well, not all of them. Managing to carry a cat home on the subway would be difficult enough, assuming you could take a cat on the subway. But a cat and a suitcase—a cat, a suitcase, her laptop computer, half a dozen boxes of files and books, and the fern, she wouldn't abandon the fern…

But Oliver came first. He needed her. And she needed him. She loved him. She always would.

"You hear that, Oliver?" she said, as fiercely, as if he could hear her. "I love you. And I'll always love you. Always, Lucas, no matter what, and—"

And, she meant Oliver, of course. The cat. Not Lucas. Not him. What was there to love? Why would she waste her tears on Lucas Vieira?

"Oh, God," Caroline whispered.

She sank to the linoleum floor, brought her knees up to her chest, buried her face in her hands.

And wept.

Sunday morning dawned gray, rainy and ugly.

Mrs. Kennelly, who had Saturdays and Mondays off, arrived at her usual time. Lucas was waiting impatiently to be told his car had arrived.

"Morning, sir," she said.

Lucas grunted a reply. She looked at him, raised an eyebrow.

"Would you like me to put on some coffee?"

Another grunt.

"Perhaps Ms. Hamilton would care for—"

"Ms. Hamilton no longer lives here," Lucas said coldly. "And where in hell is my driver?"

The house phone rang. His car had arrived.

"About time," Lucas growled, and went down to the lobby.

His driver took one glance at him and didn't even venture a

"good morning." When he reached his office, his P.A. looked up from her computer, saw his face and averted her eyes.

What the hell was wrong with everybody? Lucas thought angrily, and strode past her.

Word went around. The big man had a look to him that said, *Screw with me and heads will roll.*

Nobody was that dumb. They figured something had gone wrong with the French deal. Except, they'd seen things go wrong on other occasions and he'd never looked so—so...

"So closed off," one of his assistants whispered.

Closed off. Yes. They all agreed that was the perfect description.

The good news was that nothing had gone wrong with the French deal because when Lucas met with his people, he told them the contract would be finalized today.

One of his men, younger and newer than the others, cleared his throat.

"Then, uh, then nothing's wrong, sir?"

The look Lucas flashed made them all pull their necks lower into their shirts and shrink back in their seats around the big conference room table.

"Why would you think something was wrong?" he snarled.

No one was foolish enough to answer.

He made it through the meetings.

Made it through lunch with the Frenchman.

"Did everything work out with your lady yesterday?" the Frenchman said, over a glass of red wine.

The muscle in Lucas's jaw flexed.

"Yes."

That was all he said, but a look passed between the two men.

"Sometimes," the Frenchman said quietly, "life is not quite what we expect."

Gallic wisdom? Or the Bordeaux? Lucas wasn't sure which. He simply nodded in agreement. They finished lunch, shook hands and that was that.

He got home after seven, tired, fighting a headache that had already defeated four aspirin tablets, and trying hard to concentrate on the deal he'd concluded. The Rostov contract had been important. This one would move Vieira Financial to a level all its own, something he'd been working to achieve for years.

And he thought, *So what?*

There was a note from Mrs. Kennelly on the kitchen counter. She'd had to leave a bit early, she hoped he didn't mind. And the phone was out, some sort of problem the storm had left behind. The phone company promised things would be back to normal within the next several hours.

Lucas showered. Put on jeans, a T-shirt, mocs. Started for the stairs and, instead, walked slowly down the hall, to the guest suite.

Caroline's things were still there. Her scent, that soft vanilla fragrance, was in the air.

The ridiculous fern stood on a table near the window, but it didn't look as pathetic anymore. The fronds were green, lacy, healthy. A little TLC had revived it.

That was the thing about tender, loving care. It could work wonders.

Lucas scowled, went downstairs to the kitchen, checked to be sure Oliver had food and water. He did. So did Lucas. There were a couple of bottles of Corona in the refrigerator and a pan of something on the counter.

Lucas opened a beer, heated the pan, dumped the contents on a plate and poked at it with his fork. Oliver came into the kitchen, tail up and crooked, looked at him and said, *"Meow?"*

"Yeah," Lucas said, "hello to you, too." He stabbed at his dinner again. Looked at Oliver. "Wanna try some?"

The cat approached. Accepted a tidbit from Lucas's fingers. Chewed, swallowed, but Lucas could see the cat was just being polite.

"Me, too," he said, and dumped the rest into the trash. When he sat down again, the cat jumped into his lap.

"So," Lucas said, "how was your day?"

*"Mrrow."*

"Good. I'm glad to hear it. My day was fine, too."

*"Meow?"*

"I concluded a deal. I'm excited about it."

About as excited as the cat had been over that mouthful of food. Lucas sighed, scooped Oliver into his arms and walked into his study, sank down on a burgundy leather love seat, the cat in his lap.

"About this deal…"

The cat shut its eyes. Lucas nodded.

"To tell you the truth, I don't much give a damn, either. Crazy, isn't it? Last month, last week, I'd have been doing handstands…"

Last month, last week, he had not yet met Caroline.

And he had not yet lost her.

He cleared his throat. "The thing is," he said, "I know I should feel pleased about this French thing, but—"

But, he didn't feel much of anything.

Except alone. And lost. And painfully, brutally lonely. For Caroline, and wasn't that pathetic? Amazing, how good her masquerade had been, that he should think he missed her now.

He thought of those couple of days in the Hamptons. The joy she'd taken—the joy she'd seemed to take in the simple things they'd done. Walking the beach. Swimming in the pool. Strolling the streets of the village, hand in hand with him.

Watching the stars burn against the black silk of the night sky.

"Oh, how beautiful," she'd said.

"Beautiful," he'd agreed, but he'd been talking about her. Not just her face but her sweetness, that special quality that made her the woman she was.

The woman he'd thought she was.

Could he… Was there any possibility he'd been wrong? Heard what she'd said wrong? Misunderstood it? His throat constricted. Maybe. Maybe…

No. He'd heard the conversation. Her end of it, anyway, heard her say those things to Dani…

He gave himself a couple of seconds. Then he put Oliver on the love seat and went to his desk. He had to keep busy. That was what he always did, what he had done all his life. He'd make some notes about an investment that had caught his eye, some details he wanted researched…

What was that?

A small package sat on the edge of his desk, half-hidden by his appointment calendar. It was brightly wrapped, tied with a ribbon, festooned with a bow.

Puzzled, he tore open the wrapping paper. There was a small book inside.

*A Guide To The Stars.*

He felt a sudden tightness in his throat.

Slowly, carefully, he opened the book to the title page. And saw an inscription done in a delicate, feminine hand.

*For Lucas, in memory of a starry, starry night.*
*Your Caroline*

Lucas didn't move. Didn't blink. He just stared at the page. At what she'd written, what she'd said, how she'd signed her name. Not just "Caroline" but "Your Caroline."

How many times had he thought of her just that way? As his. His Caroline. His loving, giving, innocent Caroline. Because she was all those things.

She was.

"God," he whispered, "oh, God!"

What had he done?

To hell with what he'd overheard in that phone call. Everything he'd accused her of being, of doing, was a lie. His Caroline had never sold herself, never given herself to anyone or anything except with honesty and honor. He knew that as surely as he knew that the world was round.

Whatever he'd overheard in the phone conversation surely had a simple explanation.

Why hadn't he asked? Better still, why had he let himself leap to such an ugly conclusion?

Because he was a coward. Because he'd been terrified of putting his heart in Caroline's hands. Because he'd been afraid she'd break it.

Because it had been safer to drive her away.

He loved her.

He'd loved her from that first night when she'd dealt with him, with Leo Rostov, with Ilana Rostov, with all the unexpected nonsense he'd dumped on her, and never once flinched.

He'd loved her as soon as she'd gone into his arms, kissed him, responded to his passion with all the honesty in her heart, just as if they'd been waiting for each other all their lives.

And he had been. Waiting. For her. For his Caroline. For a love that was fearless and deep and true.

A love he had pushed away.

Could he get her back? Would she ever speak to him again, much less love him? Because she had loved him. She had loved him as he loved her until he'd said those terrible things...

*"Mrrrow,"* Oliver said from the depths of the leather love seat.

He had to get her back, but he needed a plan. He never acted on anything without a plan.

*"Mrrow,"* the cat said again.

Well, that wasn't exactly true. He hadn't planned any of what had happened with Caroline. That was how he'd won her. And how he'd lost her.

Lucas shot to his feet. Got a jacket. Five seconds later, he was gone.

Caroline stood on Fifth Avenue, Central Park behind her, Lucas's condominium building directly opposite her on the other side of the street.

It was raining. Drizzling, really, but the stuff was cold and she'd left her apartment in such a mad rush that she'd neglected to take an umbrella or a rain jacket.

What now? she kept thinking, but she couldn't come up with an answer.

She had come to get Oliver after a day of trying to reach Mrs. Kennelly with no success. She'd phoned first thing this morning but nobody answered. Voice mail didn't pick up, either.

She'd tried again. And again. And again. The phone just kept ringing. Either nobody was home or nobody was answering the phone, and that left her with a problem.

The last thing she wanted was to go to Lucas's building, take the elevator to his penthouse and have the bad luck of finding him there. Not that he meant anything to her. That was over. She just didn't want any unpleasant run-ins, that was all.

And then there was another possibility. It was even worse.

Suppose she walked into the lobby and the doorman who'd

been so friendly, the concierge who'd been so nice, told her that Mr. Vieira had left instructions to deny her entrance to his apartment?

To his life.

She wasn't sure she could have survived that.

So she'd kept phoning, pausing only long enough to take a call from Dani, who'd wanted to know if she was going to do the translating job or not.

"Not," Caroline had said, and then she'd taken a long, deep breath because, by now, it was all coming together, Lucas's fury when he found her accepting money from Dani, his fury when he'd overheard that phone call. Little things had finally added up, and she was entitled to some answers. "Dani?" she'd said. "How can you afford that townhouse? Those clothes? What, exactly, do you do for a living?"

Dani had given a low, delighted laugh.

"You're such a country mouse, Caroline! I thought you'd never figure it out. What I do for a living is just what you think I do." The laughter had left her voice. "And don't you dare sit in judgment on me!"

No, Caroline thought, she wouldn't. Who was she to sit in judgment on anyone after these last few days?

Judging Lucas, though… That was different. That he could have thought she was—she was what Dani was. Or that she was with him for his money…

Never mind.

Right now, Oliver was her sole concern. She was sure he must be scared half to death, alone and lonely as he tried to stay out of Lucas's way. She had to go and get the cat, no matter what happened in the process.

"You are not a coward," she'd told herself grimly, only a couple of hours ago.

Wrong, she thought now. She *was* a coward. Standing here, in the cold drizzle, instead of going to get her cat, proved it.

That she'd let herself think she still loved Lucas proved it, too. She didn't love him, of course. She knew that, now. She was a romantic fool, was all, and—

The light changed. Caroline took a deep breath, stepped off the curb and ran across the street. The lobby door opened.

"Ms. Hamilton," the night doorman said, "what are you doing out on an evening like—"

A sudden gust of wind all but tore the heavy door from his hand. Caroline staggered forward. Her hair whipped across her face, obscuring her vision, and she stumbled against something hard and big and unyielding...

Not "something."

Lucas.

She knew it even before he said, in a tones of disbelief, "Caroline?" She knew it because she knew the feel of him, the scent of him, and her heart began to thud.

She was a coward, after all. And a liar, because just the sound of his voice made her eyes fill with tears.

She spun away, ready to run, but his arms closed around her and he said her name again and she gave a little sob and he swung her toward him, lifted her off her feet and kissed her. For a heartbeat, she yielded to the kiss. Then, she pulled back.

"Don't," she said. "Don't you dare touch me, Lucas Vieira!"

"Caroline. Sweetheart—"

"How could you think such a thing? That I was—that I would—"

"Because I'm an idiot. That's how."

"You're worse than that." Her voice broke. "You're—you're a horrid, terrible man, and I—"

"I love you, *querida*."

"Do not '*querida*' me," she said fiercely, and slammed her fist against his shoulder.

"Caroline. I love you with all my heart. With my soul. I've loved you from the minute we met."

"Too bad, because I don't feel anything for you."

Lucas drew her to him. "Kiss me," he said, "and then tell me you don't feel anything for me."

"No. Why would I kiss you? Why would I—"

He kissed her.

"I hate you," she said, against his mouth. "I hate you, Lucas, I hate—"

He kissed her again, tasted her tears and his own.

"I despise you," she whispered, and he kissed her a third time and said he understood that she despised him, she had every right to despise him, but that didn't have to mean she didn't love him, too.

Caroline laughed. She was still crying, but she laughed anyway. How could she not? Had there ever been a man as arrogant, as impossible as her Lucas?

"I love you," he said. "I adore you."

"But you said—you believed—"

"No. I didn't. What I believed was that you were sweet and good, that you were everything I had ever dreamed of finding." Gently, he kissed her tear-dampened eyes. "I was afraid of how you made me feel, *querida*. I thought that loving you was a weakness. If I gave you my heart and you broke it…"

Caroline looked into the dark, pleading eyes of the man she loved.

"That apartment…"

Lucas nodded. "I wanted it for you." She tensed, and he shook his head. "Wait. Hear me out. It wasn't the way I made it sound." He cleared his throat. "I started out just wanting you to have a safe place to live. When we first met."

"A week ago," Caroline said with a watery laugh.

Lucas lowered his head, rested his forehead against hers.

"A lifetime ago," he said. "But then I decided against it because—because I came up with a better idea."

"What better idea?"

"I decided that the best way to keep you safe was to ask you to stay with me. To live with me." He took a steadying breath. *Deus*, he had not felt this vulnerable since the day he'd walked into his first foster home. "To become my wife."

Her heart skipped a beat but she kept her eyes on his.

"That's going a long way, just to keep a woman safe."

He smiled. "Yes," he said softly, "it is. But that's what a man does, when he loves a woman. He asks her to marry him." He tucked strands of wet hair behind her ear. "I could hardly wait to get home." He paused. This was the bad part. "I got out of the elevator and you were talking to Dani Sinclair about a job."

"She offered me a translating job. But you thought—you thought—" Her voice shook. "How could you have believed that of me?"

"What I believed was that everything I'd always known was true. That love is ephemeral. That happiness is fleeting. That what a man most loves, he loses."

Caroline took a deep breath. "You haven't lost me," she whispered, and Lucas kissed her. It was a long, sweet kiss but when it ended, he knew there was more to tell her.

"You need to know that I—that I have not led what you might call an exemplary life."

"You have. You're a good man," she said with fierce conviction.

"I was not a good child, *querida*. I told you I was poor. I didn't tell you that I was a thief. A pickpocket. That I robbed, stole money, clothing, food, anything I could. That I fought with others like savages over scraps of food. I did whatever I had to do to survive. And I learned not to trust anyone." He paused. "Sometimes, those instincts are still with me."

Tears rose in Caroline's eyes.

"It breaks my heart to think of you living like that," she whispered.

"Caroline. *Querida*, I'm not asking for your pity."

"You don't understand. Same as you, I know how the past can affect the present." Her eyes searched his. "I promised myself I'd never be like my mother. That I'd never believe in a man, trust him, only to learn that he'd deceived me."

"You can trust me. You can believe in me. I swear it." Lucas gathered Caroline close against him. "I love you. I'll always love you. All I ask is that you love me. And Oliver. He wants you back," he said solemnly. "And so do I. Marry me, sweetheart. Love me forever, as I will love you."

It wasn't a question, it was a statement. Caroline smiled through her tears. Her arrogant, assured, wonderful Brazilian lover was back.

"I love you, Lucas," she said softly. "I adore you. And I will be your wife, forever."

Lucas kissed her, to a smattering of applause.

"Congratulations," the doorman and the concierge said.

Caroline blushed. Lucas grinned. Then he swept his bride-to-be into his arms and took her home.

MODERN

## TOO PROUD TO BE BOUGHT
by Sharon Kendrick

Experience has taught Russian oligarch Nikolai Komarov that all women have their price, but he's never encountered anyone like waitress Zara Evans—a young woman too *wilful* to be bought...

## PRINCE OF SCANDAL
by Annie West

Prince Raul is furious when an archaic law forces him to marry reluctant princess Luisa Hardwicke. But outspoken Luisa challenges Raul at every turn—and he finds himself eagerly anticipating their wedding night!

## STRANGERS IN THE DESERT
by Lynn Raye Harris

Isabella, the wife Sheikh Adan thought was dead, has walked back into his life—but gone is the dutiful, pure girl he once knew! In her place is a defiant, sultry woman...who has no memory of being his wife...

## SINS OF THE PAST
by Elizabeth Power

Devastated by her lover's betrayal, Riva Singleman fled, carrying away another secret of her own. Now Damiano D'Amico is back—but will he discover the truth and demand what is rightfully his?

## On sale from 15th April 2011
## Don't miss out!

*Available at WHSmith, Tesco, ASDA, Eason
and all good bookshops*
www.millsandboon.co.uk

411/01b

## A Dark Sicilian Secret
by Jane Porter

Discovering Vittorio d'Severano's secret life, Jillian Smith's dreams of a happy-ever-after crumbled into dust… But now Vitt has returned—to claim the tiny son Jill has sworn to keep from him!

## The Beautiful Widow
by Helen Brooks

To pay off her late husband's debts, Toni George accepts a position with notorious heartbreaker Steel Landry. But she's not as immune to his potent brand of masculinity as she'd like to be…

## The Ultimate Risk
by Chantelle Shaw

Seeing Lanzo di Cosimo again makes Gina Bailey's pulse race at the memories of their heady affair. No longer a carefree innocent, can she afford to surrender in the hope that he might protect her, cherish her, for better or worse…?

## A Night With Consequences
by Margaret Mayo

Kara Redman prides herself on keeping her relationship with Blake Benedict purely professional—until a business trip to Italy proves to be her undoing! But one night with her boss has shocking consequences…

## On sale from 6th May 2011
## Don't miss out!

*Available at WHSmith, Tesco, ASDA, Eason and all good bookshops*
www.millsandboon.co.uk

# BAD BLOOD

**A POWERFUL DYNASTY, WHERE SECRETS AND SCANDAL NEVER SLEEP!**

VOLUME 1 – 15th April 2011
**TORTURED RAKE**
*by Sarah Morgan*

VOLUME 2 – 6th May 2011
**SHAMELESS PLAYBOY**
*by Caitlin Crews*

VOLUME 3 – 20th May 2011
**RESTLESS BILLIONAIRE**
*by Abby Green*

VOLUME 4 – 3rd June 2011
**FEARLESS MAVERICK**
*by Robyn Grady*

8 VOLUMES IN ALL TO COLLECT!

MILLS & BOON

www.millsandboon.co.uk

# 2 FREE BOOKS
## AND A SURPRISE GIFT

We would like to take this opportunity to thank you for reading this Mills & Boon® book by offering you the chance to take TWO more specially selected books from the Modern™ series absolutely FREE! We're also making this offer to introduce you to the benefits of the Mills & Boon® Book Club™—

- **FREE home delivery**
- **FREE gifts and competitions**
- **FREE monthly Newsletter**
- **Exclusive Mills & Boon Book Club offers**
- **Books available before they're in the shops**

Accepting these FREE books and gift places you under no obligation to buy, you may cancel at any time, even after receiving your free books. Simply complete your details below and return the entire page to the address below. You don't even need a stamp!

**YES** Please send me 2 free Modern books and a surprise gift. I understand that unless you hear from me, I will receive 4 superb new books every month for just £3.30 each, postage and packing free. I am under no obligation to purchase any books and may cancel my subscription at any time. The free books and gift will be mine to keep in any case.

Ms/Mrs/Miss/Mr _____ Initials _____

_____

Surname _____

Address _____

_____

_____ Postcode _____

E-mail _____

Send this whole page to: Mills & Boon Book Club, Free Book Offer, FREEPOST NAT 10298, Richmond, TW9 1BR